SECOND CHANCE
VALENTINE

ANNIE J. ROSE

CHAPTER 1

TRAVIS - SEVEN YEARS AGO

I could have put the bottle down.

I could have done it. Put the bottle down. Stop drinking liquor. Get a liter of water into me, and go to bed. It was what I should have done. All of these actions would have been the right thing to do. To save myself, my reputation, and everyone else. Just stop drinking.

But I didn't. If for no other reason than it was what was expected of me. At a time like that, I was so stressed that I leaned into my darkest fears, my darkest worries. I was afraid of becoming just like my parents. Just like everyone in my hometown thought I would turn out. A useless waste of a human being. A drunk and drug addict bent on self-destruction and willing to take anyone else down with me.

Including Carrie.

I needed more time with Carrie, but it was impossible. Between the pre-med classes that were taking up all my energy and the work that was paying for the classes I was taking, there was no time for her. I needed her, and I couldn't have her. When I did have time, those rare moments when I wasn't at work, wasn't in class, or wasn't passed out asleep whenever I got back to the joke of an apartment, she was usually in class herself.

So I drank.

It was the only thing to do to pass the time while I was still awake. I desperately wanted to sleep, but my eyes wouldn't stay closed. I had energy. I felt like I could run a marathon. I had mountains of energy, which was unlike every other waking hour of my life when I felt like I was dragging a three-ton ball and chain.

But the thing I wanted to do most, the thing I really needed, was to see Carrie. She was home, but probably sleeping by now. It was past midnight, and she had texted me good night hours before. She had 6:00 a.m. classes, and she definitely needed her rest. But I needed her. For once, I wanted to be selfish and have her. Even though I knew this would cause us both to drag the next day, it would be worth it for her.

Tired Travis was Tomorrow Travis's problem. For now, it was time for me to do something for me. And for her too.

I stumbled out to my car and jammed the key in the ignition. A little voice in the back of my head was screaming something about my ability to drive, but my need to see Carrie was overruling everything. I hit the gas and tore out onto the road.

Thankfully, her parents only lived a short drive away. It was what we told ourselves to make things okay. We wouldn't drift apart if I went to college just outside Monroe. If I stayed in Wisconsin, we could make it work easily. And staying so close to town would mean it was just a little different than high school.

Boy, were we wrong.

I turned onto the backstreets, roads I had driven down

since before I even had my real license. It would take a couple of minutes more, but it would avoid speed traps and cops. If I could just make it to her, it would be okay. I'd sneak into her room and curl up with her. We'd wake up in each other's arms, and she would skip class. It would be perfect. We deserved it. As long as her parents didn't find out. As long as her dad didn't hear me.

I caught myself swerving once or twice and checked the windows to make sure I wasn't being followed. The coast was clear. I felt bad about driving, but it was too late now. I was already on the road. I was almost there.

Soon, I was on her street. I slowed down and pulled up to the sidewalk, parking a house down so I wouldn't be as obvious. If her dad saw my car in the morning, he might suspect. So, I hid myself. I was proud of my sneakiness when I shut the door too loud. I winced, looking around to see if anyone was around. No lights came on. No one came out. It was quiet on the suburban street.

Staggering toward her house, I had tunnel vision for her room. Carrie slept in the bed just below the window on the second floor, on the right-hand side. I'd snuck in there before. Though, I was sober then. It required climbing the porch, and then the roof to get to her window. I felt like Spider-Man when I did it. I was filled with liquid confidence.

I began to climb the porch and slipped. My foot banged against the side of the house, and I froze, hanging from the roof of the porch. My legs kicked as I heard something inside. A light went on in the living room. I began to scramble, throwing one leg up to get it on top of the roof. The door jiggled, and I could see the curtains move as I tried to move my body up and on top.

Then I slipped again.

3

I crashed into the bushes, my hip banging off the banister. Thorns scratched my face and arms. For a moment, all I could think was that I was mad at myself for not wearing a jacket. Then I heard it—the big booming voice of an angry father. Mr. Jacobs was hollering at me from the edge of the porch. I looked up at his twisted, angry face and grimaced.

"Jesus Christ, Travis, I almost shot you," he yelled as I scrambled to my feet, stumbling and falling as I tried to make it back to the front porch steps.

"I'm sorry, Mr. Jacobs. I'm just here to see Carrie," I slurred. I could hear it. My letters were running together, and the sound was one slow jumble rather than a coherent phrase. I pursed my lips and then opened them to try again.

"Are you drunk?" Mr. Jacobs asked, cutting me off.

I was stunned that he could tell. I shook my head and nearly fell backward.

"Yeah," I said. "I guess so."

"Did you drive here?" he asked, looking over at my car, which I now realized wasn't as expertly hidden as it was parked halfway in the road, with the front right tire sitting on the curb of the sidewalk.

"I was safe," I muttered.

"The hell you were," Mr. Jacobs said. "I always knew you would turn out like your old man."

His voice was full of venom, and my eyes burned into him. It was the worst insult he could lob at me, and as angry as I was at him for it, I was also hurt. I had known him for a long time, and I knew he didn't like me, but to say that...

"I just want to see Carrie," I said again.

"It will be a cold day in hell when I let you see my daughter again," he said. He had stepped down off the porch now. Mrs. Jacobs had come to the door and taken

4

something from him before he stepped down. Then she had looked at me, shook her head, and closed the door.

Mr. Jacobs was mere feet from me. He was only wearing a white T-shirt and pajama pants. His fists were clenching. I realized he wanted to hit me.

"You were never good enough for my daughter," he grumbled. "If I ever found out you drove Carrie while you were drunk, I swear I will kill you. Now call someone to pick you up and go throw away someone else's future. Leave my daughter alone."

With that, he turned and stomped back to his house. Slamming the door shut, he snapped the light off, and I was left in the darkness of his front yard. So many emotions were bubbling through my chest, and I couldn't focus on a single one of them. Part of me wanted to scream, part of me wanted to sob. Part of me wanted to go beat the door down and tell him I was only here because I loved his daughter so much, I felt like I couldn't breathe without her.

But he was right. I would just screw her up more than I already had. It was what my family did.

I let out a roar of frustration as I slammed the car door shut and jammed key after key at the ignition until I got the right one. I didn't remember how I got back home, but when I woke up in the morning, I was passed out on the couch and could see where I'd parked it mostly in the parking space in front of the building. It was a tight fit for the car next to it but a miracle it wasn't crashed into it. The front tires, however, were up on the curb.

This was about all I could see clearly before the blinding headache ripped through my frontal cortex, and I winced in pain. The light was overwhelming, and I dove my head into the corner of the couch, pulling the throw pillow overtop of me. Everything hurt.

I was ashamed I'd driven like that. I wanted to be a doctor, and here I was making the stupidest, most reckless decision of my life. I was going to ruin my career before it even got started. Just like Dad would have.

It was careless, and I wanted to go move the car to hide the evidence and then bury myself in my bed until the shame went away. But I knew it never would. The words Carrie's father said haunted me, rattling around in my brain and daring me to think it was a dream. I knew it wasn't, no matter how much I wished it was.

He said I was going to ruin her life, and he was right. I was a screwup just like my parents were. I wasn't good enough for her; I knew it, and so did he. The only person who didn't seem to get it was Carrie herself. She loved me and would do everything and anything to make me happy and that's what was dangerous. She would ruin her life for me if I asked her to. I couldn't let that happen.

I lay there for a little while, trying to will the headache away. It wouldn't go. Nothing was going to stop that pounding but time and food and water. I got up, took a few aspirins, and got myself a huge glass of water. Immediately after drinking some of it, I was in the bathroom puking up my guts. At some point, I passed out and woke up, feeling a little better but still terrible. And still with those words ringing in my head.

I shuffled into the living room and grabbed my phone. I knew what I had to do. Pulling up her messages hurt so much worse than I was expecting it to. I typed the words I knew I didn't believe but had to say. I told her that I didn't love her anymore and that I was done. We were done. And I was leaving town and never, ever coming back.

I waited to hit Send until I went into my room and packed my things. I grabbed as much as I could load into the car and then wrote my parents a note. They wouldn't care. They hadn't cared about me in a long time.

I hit Send as I turned the ignition over. Pulling away, the car thumped as it came off the curb, and I grimaced. It would never happen again. None of this would ever happen again.

CHAPTER 2

CARRIE

The sun in my eyes woke me up, and I groaned as I rolled over to turn my head away from the window. I could tell by how bright the light was I had slept in far longer than I'd intended to. It was hard not to. School was so stressful the last semester, and it left me perpetually short on sleep. Now that it was winter break, I was going to milk every second to relax.

Most of my professors had given projects earlier in the semester that could stand in for our final exam grade if we were happy with what we were scoring in the course. Taking advantage of that and getting my only written final done at the beginning of the week meant I'd finished up several days before many of the other students.

This included Travis. He was still wading through studying for his intense pre-med finals and was feeling a lot of stress. But I knew he was going to knock them out of the park. He was brilliant and the hardest-working person I knew. His grades were glowing, and he worked full-time to put himself through school.

All that came at a price, though. Unfortunately, that price was our time together.

Feeling the strain in my relationship with Travis hadn't made the stress and exhaustion of the semester any easier. We didn't get to see each other anywhere near as much as I would want to. It always felt like we would never not be able to make time for each other. After all, we were once completely wrapped up in one another and could barely go a few hours apart without calling or texting.

These last few months had challenged that. We were studying such different things, our schedules never lined up, and we didn't share any classes. We were always busy with studies and projects, not to mention his work, and it got harder and harder to spend any time together.

I missed him so much, but I was also incredibly proud of him. Travis was going against the odds in just about every way a person could. Since the time I was sixteen years old, he was my world, but I knew from the beginning not everybody shared my view of him. I saw a strong, sweet, caring, and driven guy who I just knew would grow up to be an amazing man and doctor one day.

The rest of our small town had a much narrower view of him. They saw Travis King, the son of a couple whose reputation was infamous around our town. The stories of what they had done were scattered and varied, and there was no way all of them could possibly be true. Unfortunately, some of them were. And even a drop of truth poisoned everyone's view of the Kings family.

It trickled down to their only son, and he'd grown up with no chance of getting out from under their negative reputation. He was prejudged from childhood, and there was nothing he could do to change it.

I didn't care. It didn't matter to me who his parents were. I only cared about who he was, and the person I knew was amazing. This was why no matter how much my parents tried to push for me to end our relationship, I wouldn't. Nothing would make me break up with him. Things were hard, but they would get better. We were only sophomores in college, and both of us were trying to juggle heavy course loads. Travis had piled his job on top of that and was pushing through pre-med studies.

His schedule was backbreaking, and it left a little time for anything else. I understood that. It wouldn't last forever. Eventually, we would both come out the other end, and we would have the future we'd always planned together.

I was really hoping winter break would be a good chance for us to reconnect. As soon as he was done with his finals, we would be able to be together more. The thought must have really been on my mind even as I fell asleep because as I came more into consciousness, I vaguely remembered a dream I had the night before where I heard his voice but didn't know where he was.

I lay there trying to remember the rest of the dream, but it didn't come to me. Stretching out against my covers, I reached under my pillow for my phone. I wanted to call Travis and wish him luck on his finals. When I looked at my screen, I couldn't help but smile.

He had beaten me to the punch. There was already a text message from him waiting for me. I rolled onto my back and snuggled down deeper into the blankets to enjoy the warmth for a little longer while I read the message. But when I opened it, a chill ran through me.

My smile disappeared. I had to read through the message over and over to make sure I was seeing it correctly. It couldn't actually say what I thought it did. Travis couldn't be breaking up with me. Not like that. It didn't make any sense.

Sitting upright, I tried to call him. Panic was making me shake, and it was hard to get the buttons to cooperate. Finally, I managed to hit the call button on his contact listing, but it didn't do any good. The phone didn't even ring. It went straight to voicemail. I called five more times, and five more times there was no ring, just the generic statement asking me to leave a message.

His phone must have been turned off. My voice trembled as I left him a message asking him to call me. My feet were already on the floor before I hung up, and I didn't even bother to put a bathrobe on over the sweatsuit I slept in before running out of my room and down the stairs.

I could hear my mother in the kitchen and smell the bacon she was cooking for breakfast. Obviously, they were trying to accommodate my extra hours of sleep. I didn't care. There wasn't a question in my mind about what led Travis to sending that message to me. I only wanted to know how.

My mother turned around from the stove and smiled at me as I came into the kitchen.

"Morning, honey," she said. "You're sure in a rush this morning. Did you sleep well?"

I ignored everything she said and crossed the room in three long strides to hold the phone up in front of her face, displaying the text message. She withdrew slightly, taking a step back from me.

"Do you know anything about this?" I demanded.

"What is that?" she asked.

"A message from Travis breaking up with me. You don't know anything about it? Any reason why he might do that out of nowhere?"

"No," she said. "I don't know anything about it. I have no idea what goes on in that boy's mind."

I didn't believe her. The swipe at Travis was enough to prove that she not only didn't care about what was happening but was happy about it. A second later, I heard my father coming down the stairs, and I ran out of the kitchen to meet him.

"Do you know anything about this?" I demanded, showing him the text.

"What do you mean?" he asked.

"Don't lie to me. I know you have something to do with this. What did you do?"

"Don't talk to me like that, young lady," he said fiercely, glaring at me through narrowed eyes.

"Don't talk to me like a child," I retorted. "Travis broke up with me out of nowhere, and I know it was because of you. What did you say to him? What did you do?"

My father stepped down off the bottom stair and walked around me toward the kitchen. I followed him, the anger building up inside me.

"Maybe you shouldn't be asking me what I did, and wonder what *he* did," Dad said.

"What's that supposed to mean?"

"He showed up here last night drunk, belligerent, and out of control. He drove himself here, Carrie. I don't think I need to tell you how I feel about someone who would not only drink underage but drive in that condition. That boy is just like his parents, exactly like we've always told you. You should see this for what it is—a blessing. He was never good enough for you," Dad said.

Now I realized what I thought was a dream of hearing Travis's voice was *actually* hearing him outside the house when he came the night before. It made my stomach turn and even more fury rush up my spine. I couldn't believe it had gotten to this point. They were always awful about him, but to think they had actually driven him away pushed me over the edge of my control.

"How dare you?" I screamed. "I am so tired of you not trusting me to know my own worth or to be able to make my own decisions about my relationship. In case you haven't noticed yet, I'm an adult. I can make my own decisions, and I'm sick of you getting in my way."

My father glared at me again, sticking his finger out toward me like he was scolding a toddler.

"What did I say about the way you are speaking to me?" he asked.

"This is such bullshit!" I shouted and saw his eyes go wide. Never in my life had I used language like that in front of my father, much less in a statement going directly to him. But I didn't care. I had gone past any point of being able to control myself and was completely freaking out. "You act like you know everything and are so much better than everyone else. I'm so tired of it, of you always painting Travis with the same brush as his parents. You don't know him. You never have."

I turned my back on my father and ran for the front door. I was proud of myself for not letting the tears stinging in the back of my eyes fall while I was talking to him. I didn't want to give him the satisfaction of seeing me cry. Even though it was the only thing I wanted to do. Running out to the front door to my car, I didn't care that it was cold, and I wasn't even wearing shoes. The sharp chill of the frost bit into the bare soles of my feet, but it didn't matter. I didn't have the time to think about it.

I needed to get to Travis. Even as I turned the key I'd snatched from the hook beside the front door, I had my phone in my hand and was trying to call him again. Just like before, it went straight to voicemail. I left another message, telling him I was on the way to his house.

Hanging up the call, I threw my phone into the passenger seat and drove straight to his parents' house. I jumped out of the car and ran for the door, knocking on it far too hard. His father came to it and stared out at me through bleary eyes.

"Carrie?" he said, rubbing his hand down over his face like he was trying to wake himself up. "What are you doing here?"

"Is he here?" I asked.

"Who?"

"Travis," I shouted. "Is Travis here?"

Mr. King shook his head. "No."

"Where is he?"

He shrugged. "I don't know. He got in late last night, and this morning he loaded up his car and left."

"When?" He looked like he was falling asleep on his feet, and I took a step closer to him. "When? When did he leave?"

My louder voice broke through, and he opened his eyes again. "Early. I was getting ready to turn in. He left a note saying he was going. Just got packed and left."

I felt shell-shocked as I backed away from the house. Without saying anything else, I got back in my car and drove home. By the time I got there, there was nothing I could do to stop the tears flowing down my face. Parking in front of the house, I pulled the key out of the ignition, dropped my head, and began sobbing.

CHAPTER 3

TRAVIS - PRESENT DAY

"This can't be right," I said.

"Wait, let me see," my advisor, a lovely lady named Claire, said. She pulled the papers back in front of her, adjusted her horn-rimmed glasses, and read over them, her lips moving with the words, then handed them back. "No, that's correct."

I sat in stunned silence for a moment, looking over the papers. The words were there, and I could read them, but it was all too much. It was like I was being pranked. I secretly wondered who was recording me and from where and for which crappy social media app where pranking people was still a thing. When no one jumped out from behind the window curtain or slammed the door open shouting I had been the subject of a failed attempt at minor celebrity, I shook my head and stood up.

"Thank you, Claire."

She smiled. "Good luck, Travis, and enjoy your trip back home!"

Home. As if that was a word that I associated with the place I'd grown up.

Disgusted, I tried my best to keep my composure until I left the office and made it to an empty courtyard. It was there, in the view of several younger med students and a very upset flock of geese, that I swore so much that I was fairly sure I invented several new words that could make a sailor blush. I kicked at nothing and slammed my hands to my sides as I muttered and yelled for the thirty seconds I was going to allow myself to react. After that, I had to have composure. I had to figure out what exactly I was going to do.

I didn't want to go back to Monroe, ever. It was in my past, and yet, no matter how much I felt like it was gone for good, it kept showing back up in my life. Two years ago, both my parents had died in an accident, and I'd had to fly into the next town over to sign a bunch of papers and make sure their remains were taken care of. Not that I wanted anything to do with it, but it was my responsibility.

So was their house, which they'd left me. I had brief thoughts about renting it out and turning it into a source of income, but it needed repairs, and I didn't have the time or inclination. So it sat, empty. And I frankly hadn't even thought about it. I quietly continued to pay taxes for the property and kept the water and electricity on. I was set on fixing it if I ever found the time, which I never did.

What my parents actually left me was a bunch of things I paid for and got no use out of. It was so on brand for them. They left me problems and no easy solutions. Like always, it was going to be up to me to make something out it. Out of myself.

Now this. Now I was going to spend the next three years of my life in Monroe doing my residency. What a kick in the teeth that was.

Claire, bless her, had tried to put a spin on it. When she first handed me the papers, she said it would be a homecoming. Basically, the local hospital needed my help. And since I was a local, it would come in extremely handy with the patients who generally resisted out of town practitioners. I knew that all too well. The people of Monroe were nice, but skeptical, and generally unwilling to accept that new people could be good people. And once you had proven yourself or your family to be not good people, there was no way back in. Even if you were just a kid.

Finally, a little calmer, I made my way back to my apartment to pack. The last time I lived near Monroe, I was shacking up in a crappy campus apartment in the college town next door with three roommates. Aside from the first six months of school in Tennessee, I hadn't lived with anyone else since. I had made it this way a long time ago with the intention of never seeing the great land of cheese ever again. But now, I had just a few days to pack everything, cancel my lease, and make my way by car all the way back to start at the small hospital in town on Monday. It was insane.

I knew that I could get it done, just like I got everything else done by sheer force of will. When I'd left Monroe, and everything it had behind, I became an entirely different person. At least I felt like one. Away from anyone who ever knew me or my fuck-up parents, I was able to establish a new life. It was a boring life, sure, filled with almost nothing but work and school, but it was respectable. It was decent. It was mine. No one would dare call me unworthy of the life I had. I worked my fingers and my mind to the absolute max for it.

As I got inside my apartment, I realized I would have to

stop at a store for more clothes. Tennessee didn't have what I would call a real winter. It got cold sometimes, sure, but nothing like the bitter, snowy craziness of Wisconsin. I was known to be the guy everyone thought was crazy, walking around town in a short-sleeved shirt in winter. But I was used to far worse. Back in Monroe it would have been a picnic day when the people of southern Tennessee were bundling up in coats that made them look like the Stay-Puft Marshmallow Man.

I began throwing things into duffel bags and suitcases. Of course I had to find the suitcases first because I hadn't seen them since I put them away when I moved in. Vacations were things other people took, and even when I had time off from studies, I was working. I never had a need to whip out a suitcase and pack up my socks and underwear, at least not in the six years I'd had that apartment.

Six years of sobriety. Six years of non-stop school. Six years of missing Carrie.

Of course I missed her. She was the love of my life. Even still, she appeared in my dreams. They were more like nightmares now, though. The comfort of sleeping was warm and fulfilling, but waking up was the disappointment and heartache that nearly drove me back to the bottle, time and time again. But I refrained. I would let myself do anything but use alcohol or drugs to cope. I could pace around the house and yell. I could exercise, which I did often. And I could cook elaborate meals for one, or best yet, go to a meeting or call my sponsor. But I would not drink or otherwise alter my mind with chemicals.

I would not be my parents.

I tried to not think about her and focused on packing. I needed as much done in one day as possible and throwing my clothes into suitcases was at least something positive. I would probably need a moving truck for the furniture and would need to be able to tow my car too. It was becoming a bigger headache the more I thought about it, but it was my own fault. I wanted the early residency. I'd fought for it. This was the hand I was dealt, and there was no use bitching about it.

I had to deal with it how I dealt with every other hand. By playing it and bluffing until I had a plan. Then executing that plan to the best of my will.

Friends weren't something I had many of, but I did have a few acquaintances from school. I could call a few that I knew and ask if they could help me load stuff into the truck. I opened my phone and texted a couple of them to float the question, then made a reservation for the moving truck. I was going to have to make the run to the store as soon as I was done packing my clothes and everything I could get into boxes and totes I already had.

This was already becoming a bigger hassle than I wanted, and I was beginning to hate myself for signing up for the early opportunity. But then again, I likely would have ended up there anyway. It was my luck. I had run from my past for so long, it was bound to catch up with me sooner or later. I was going to have to go back and address the things I had done wrong and atone for them at some point, or at least allow for the consequences of my actions to take hold.

Seven years was a long time away. Maybe there wouldn't be any consequences. It wasn't like I had done much personally to have to make up for. And with my residency at the hospital being a respectable job, maybe people would just leave me alone about my parents.

Who knew? It was going to be a crapshoot how anyone took to me showing back up, and frankly, at the end of the day I didn't care. There was only one person I cared about seeing and how they reacted to me being back and that was Carrie. I couldn't imagine she would be happy to see me after everything that happened.

I'd left her, with almost no explanation. I changed my phone when I got to Tennessee and didn't give anyone from Monroe the number. It took the police tracking me down to even tell me my parents had died. No one had contact with me in years, much less Carrie, who I assumed stopped trying when I changed my number. It was the whole point. I'd needed to cut her completely out of my life.

For her own good.

It certainly wasn't for mine. I spent a year indulging in more drinking, partying, doing everything I could to ignore the pain and the loneliness I'd suffered when I ran away. The shame of it all.

I still believed that I'd made the right call to save her from even more heartache. Right down to my core, I believed that I did the right thing for her, and for myself. One day she would have figured it out and left me, and where would I be then? I would have been completely dependent on her, and she would eventually grow tired of it and run off. I would be in far worse shape than I ended up in, and she would have wasted years on me. I did what needed to be done. I let her succeed, without me. And I went away. Presumably for good.

Only now I was coming back, and I had to come to grips with the fact that I still missed her. I missed her every single day of my life, and it was entirely likely I would run into her. How would she react? I knew the answer to that. I knew it would kill me to see her do it. But it would be good for her to get it off her chest. And good for me because it would help me move on. I still loved her, and I always would. But the damage had been done.

I groaned, done with packing for that moment, and flopped down onto my bed. It was going to be a long night.

CHAPTER 4

CARRIE

I kept my eyes closed for the first few seconds after waking up. Stretching my legs deeper into my favorite flannel sheets I had just put fresh on my bed the night before, I spread my toes and enjoyed the feeling of the soft fabric against my skin.

Reaching over my head with both arms, I pressed my hands to the headboard and groaned a little as the stretch woke up my muscles. The sunlight coming through the window touched my face. It was a peaceful, pleasant way to start a good morning.

Too peaceful and pleasant.

My eyes snapped open, and I looked through the window. The sunlight was much too bright, the sun too high in the sky. I scrambled over to the side of the bed and grabbed my phone from the nightstand, yanking it off the charger so I could look at it. My alarm had somehow been silenced, and I way overslept.

Nothing said my day was going to hell like waking up late. My daily routine was set in stone. It had to be to make sure everything got done and I was able to juggle all the different aspects of my life effectively. This meant on a Tuesday morning I should have been up before the sun making breakfast and getting Amelia's lunch packed before packing my own lunch and doing early prep for the dinner I would finish cooking when we both got home.

Instead, I threw the covers off and tumbled out of bed so fast I almost fell. I managed to catch myself at the last second before face-planting into the rug and ran for the bathroom.

Sleeping in just wasn't something I did. My alarm went off at the same time every morning, and I never hit the snooze. I got up early religiously and followed the same schedule for each day of the week. Now I was already off by a couple of hours, and I didn't know how I was going to scramble and catch up.

I threw myself into the shower and attempted to multi-task by washing my body with the lather from shampooing my hair, but I couldn't stand it, so I followed up with the fastest possible cleaning with whatever bath gel I grabbed when I reached indiscriminately onto the hanging metal shelf.

As I washed, I realized I had probably grabbed one of Amelia's bottles. The scent was intensely sweet and reminiscent of cotton candy dipped in some sort of fruit syrup. Perfect for a six-year-old—not so much for that six-year-old's mother. Sickly sweet was going to have to do for the day. Maybe I would pull it off.

I rinsed and launched myself out of the shower and back into my room so I could throw on my bathrobe and go wake Amelia up. As I rushed down the hallway, however, I realized I wouldn't need to. I could hear the sound of cartoons coming from the living room. When I went in, I found Amelia curled up in the corner of the couch with a blanket pooled around her like a nest. She was watching morning cartoons as she munched through a bowl of cereal.

For a moment, I tried to be surprised at finding her that way. But I couldn't be. My little girl was smart and had always been independent, so it wasn't that unusual to see that she had taken control of the mourning herself.

"Look at you," I said. "Already up and having breakfast."

She nodded. "Shouldn't you have been up a while ago?"

I let out a sigh. "Yes. I should have been. Something happened to my alarm. I'm going to grab something to eat and get your lunch packed. Finish up your cereal and go get dressed for school." I leaned down to drop a kiss on her head. "Come on. We can't get you to school late."

I went into the kitchen and slipped a couple of pieces of bread into the toaster. Pushing the lever down, I moved to the refrigerator to start taking out the elements of Amelia's lunch while my bread toasted. Mastering multitasking was one of the skills I honed after becoming a mother.

By the time I got most of Amelia's lunch packed, my toast had popped up from the toaster. Grabbing out the slices, I slathered them with butter, topped it with peanut butter in the name of protein, and stuffed half of one in my mouth. I chewed while making the rest of Amelia's lunch, then moved on to my own. The last bite slid down my throat with a swig of the cold brew coffee I poured from the pitcher in my refrigerator just as I finished up packing my lunch.

With that wrapped up, I rushed back toward my bedroom. It was like I could feel the morning slipping by. I got dressed in record time and threw my still-wet hair up into a ponytail. Scooping my makeup into my cosmetic bag,

I stuffed my feet into shoes and headed for the living room again.

My daughter was dressed and back sitting on the couch watching her cartoons when I got there. I did a quick check of her outfit without saying anything. I liked to encourage her to be as independent as she wanted to be, but I hadn't quite brought myself to be the type of mother that would willingly send her off to school in whatever conglomeration of garments she happened to select in the morning.

It was one of the smooth, though somewhat rare, mornings when she went with the outfit I'd laid out for her. It was something I did every night. I picked out an outfit for her and laid it out on the rocking chair in the corner of her bedroom. It signified the end of our nighttime reading routine and gave us the first step in getting the next day underway.

There was always the chance she would wake up in the morning with no intention of putting that outfit on. but it didn't bother me as long as she kept her attitude in check and replaced the clothes with something acceptable. The fact that both of those qualifications were falling into place made me at once a bit more optimistic about the day.

We zipped ourselves into our coats and piled into the car, lunches in hand. I got Amelia to school just as the students were scrambling inside with their teaching assistants. The bright-eyed, young-faced assistants were tasked with meeting all the students outside the school in the morning, then escorting them to their classrooms.

Later they would escort them to and from lunch and recess before reprising their morning responsibilities in reverse by bringing the children out to meet their parents at pickup. All the little trains of children winding through the school and gathering in distinct clusters eliminated anyone going inside and minimized risk, but I didn't want to think of it that way.

I preferred to just accept my little girl's happy morning kisses, then savor a few seconds of watching her skip off to her friends and head into school for the day. I was so proud of her. She was truly the light of every day of my life.

As soon as she was inside, I made my way to work. I parked in my designated spot behind the bakery with a renewed sense of thankfulness for the people I'd hired to help me run my business. My bakery was warm, comforting, and homey. My staff helped me keep it that way.

Like every other aspect of my life, the bakery ran smoothly and on a firmly set routine. My two helpers were truly godsends who were there to balance out the rocky start to the day.

Just like every morning, they were there to open the bakery before I arrived. And this was the entire point of hiring them. I knew I wouldn't be able to be there to open the bakery up early enough for commuters and other early morning people to come in for breakfast or a special treat to bring into the office.

If I couldn't open until later in the morning, my potential business would be slashed. I wanted to be there to open it up in the morning, but I had Amelia. She came first. She always did and always would. My daughter was my priority, so I found a way to make things work.

It allowed me to spend some extra time in the evening setting up the baked goods that would end up filling the display case the next morning. I prepared everything as much as I could and set up the trays so all my employees had to do was put them in the oven when they opened first thing in the morning. That way they would be fully stocked, and I could still be absolutely confident in the quality of what filled the shelves.

I entered the bakery through the back door, but instead of heading straight to the kitchen or out to the front, I made my way to the office. It was important I kept up with the administrative responsibilities of the bakery rather than just letting myself get lost in baking and creating delicious treats.

I hung my coat and bag up on the coat rack in the back corner of the office, then sat down in front of my computer to get into the swing of things. This included checking over my schedule to make sure I was on track for any bolt or custom orders, checking my email, responding to any messages I might have gotten, and setting up schedules and plans of attack for everything that needed to be made that week.

Now that I was at work, I was feeling more like I was finding my feet in the snowball of a morning. At the end of the school day my mother would pick Amelia up and bring her here to the bakery so she could spend the rest of the afternoon with me. There was a little desk in the office where she could work on her homework and a couch where she could read or take a nap.

But usually, Amelia ended up in the kitchen with me. She loved to bake and seemed to be devoting her young brain to absorbing every one of my recipes and techniques. She said she wanted to learn them so she could make them for her children one day. There was never any suggestion of her taking over the bakery. I had a feeling there were other dreams brewing in her head.

Whatever the future held for my little girl, I cherished the afternoons we spent in the bakery together. I would stand at one part of the counter making up the batches of bread, cupcakes, cookies, quiches, and other goodies that would fill the display cases. Amelia found her own spot and worked with the scrap pieces of dough and little bowls of batter I gave her.

When I finished my morning office work, I crossed through the kitchen on my way to the front of the bakery. On my way through the door, I grabbed one of the aprons hanging just inside the kitchen and tied it into place.

Parker and Maggie, my two helpers, grinned at me as I walked in. I checked in with them and scanned the display cases to see if anything needed to be restocked. The three of us would all work together through the morning until Parker left for his afternoon classes. Then it would just be Maggie and me until Amelia got there.

In the evening after I closed up, my daughter and I would go back home, have dinner together, and drift toward bedtime. Then the next morning, it started all over again.

It was a simple life, but it was a good one.

CHAPTER 5

TRAVIS

One of the big upsides to working at Monroe General, if you could call it an upside, was that as a resident, they covered my living expenses. Or at least the bulk of them. I was put up in an apartment just off the hospital campus within walking distance if I didn't mind a little exercise, which I didn't. I also had a stipend put onto a card that I could use in the cafeteria that was good for at least a lunch or dinner every day I worked. It would help me save a good bit of money while I was there, though for those perks they expected quite a lot.

I wasn't afraid of the challenge, nor was I going to back down from hard work, but this hospital was in a lot of trouble. Recent overloads of patients and lack of staff or resources meant that everyone was exhausted all the time. There was always a crunch to hire new nurses and train them fast enough so that they got the hang of working there before they inevitably quit or transferred out due to the stress and poor management. It was a high-paced, intense environment, and with the closing of a local hospital about ten miles out of town, we were expecting our work to get more difficult.

This was good, though, as far as I thought, at least for me. It meant I would be on my toes and busy all the time. There wouldn't be time for me to get all morose and think about Carrie if I didn't barely have enough time to remember to breathe. My first day had started hot, and I was already deep into the learning curve of the hospital by the time I checked out and went back to the apartment. It was a shorter shift, just to get me used to the way things ran, but short meant eight hours. The warning was the next day was going to be much, much more. I was ready.

Hiring movers to put my stuff in the apartment was something I never thought I would do, but I was so glad I had. Everything was inside and waiting for me when I got home from that first day, and all I had to do was shower, eat, and put sheets on the bed before I crashed. My alarm was set well before I had to be in the next day, and I wanted a good eight hours, thinking it might be the only time I got it for a while. But when the alarm went off, I had already been awake for some time, too nervous and excited to get the day going.

On my way home from my first day, I'd noticed a cute little bakery close by. It was something I thought I would enjoy every morning, if I could get myself out of bed and get a workout in. What was the purpose of keeping myself in shape if I couldn't enjoy a donut or something sweet? Unfortunately, this was going to have to wait for another day to start the tradition. I had to get into work early enough to beat my boss in.

Dr. Jones was everything I wanted to be when I passed my residency. Middle-aged and revered by the staff, he was kind and brilliant and compassionate. He was also the type of man who didn't take crap from anyone. People who he found to be lazy or inconsiderate of their patients were often met with a stern look and a very select few but extremely demoralizing words that cut a person down to the quick. If you didn't shape up after Dr. Jones spoke to you, you either transferred out or found another profession. But most people simply just got better. By sheer force of will, Dr. Jones made everyone around him better at their jobs.

I spent much of that first day hearing stories about the man, and then shadowing him for a while showed me they were likely all true. He was impeccable and authoritative while still being approachable and amiable to patients. He had the kind of nature that patients never argued with him and took his advice as the gospel that it was. So, my desire to impress him was at an all-time high for me.

Forgoing the sugary sweets, I went directly into work, beating Dr. Jones there by ten or so minutes. When he saw me as he walked down the hall, I saw his eyebrows raise over the gold-rimmed glasses that sat perennially on the end of his nose. If he wasn't impressed, he was surprised to see me. I got the feeling that arriving early was the sole calling card of Dr. Jones himself.

"Travis, good to see you so early," he said. "We have much to do today. I hope you got some sleep."

"I did," I lied. "Ready to go." At least that part was the truth.

The hospital was small, but newly redone. The state had invested in it, and with all the investment that went there, the other local hospital transferring their patients and business to us seemed logical if cruel. Some of the people coming in had to drive over an hour to get to us. Dr. Jones was empathetic and went out of his way more than once early in the morning to make sure people knew there were closer options rather than to come to us.

A brief break saw him usher me to a small breakroom just beyond the nurses' station. Inside was a refrigerator packed to the brim with sodas, sports drinks, cold coffees, and the like. A hot coffee maker was right beside it, and as soon as we were in the room, Dr. Jones poured himself a cup of unmodified black coffee and began to put it down in liberal gulps.

"There are various sodas and things in the fridge if you don't want coffee. I see to it that it's stocked every day. I made them get rid of the vending machine a year ago," he said.

"Thank you, that's very nice," I said.

"It's weak of me. Most of the drinks in there I would tell my patients to swear off for their health, but I understand nurses need their sugar fix. Else I raise their scorn."

I laughed. "Coffee is fine too," I said. "Though, I can't quite drink it black."

Dr. Jones cracked a smile. "You know, I barely taste it anymore. It's become such a routine for me to come in and put away a mug or two of it that they switched to decaf for a month and I didn't even notice. I stopped putting the creamer in it out of lack of time years ago, and if I didn't put the cream in, I couldn't bear to just dump sugar in. So black it is."

"I might be a few years away from that," I said. "I'm still a pansy and need my coffee to be brown. Closer to light brown."

"You'll get there," he said sagely. "Sooner than you think."

With that, he finished his mug and reached for the carafe just as I finished with it. He poured another mug and leaned against the counter. There was something else I had been told about him. He never sat, not unless he was with a patient. He preferred to stay up, moving. There were nursing assistants who swore they saw him sleeping that way on break one time, casually propped up against the counter, coffee mug in hand at his chest, sound asleep.

I could believe it.

"So, you said you chose pediatrics. May I ask why?" he asked. "Not a criticism, mind you. I also chose pediatrics many, many years ago. I am always curious about other people's journeys."

"Well," I began, realizing that this was a big moment. I could impress the boss, or I could say something that could make my life harder. It was possible the next three years of my residency could ride on that conversation. I decided to just go with blunt honesty. "I didn't think I was going to, frankly. I didn't think I was great with children, or that I wanted to be. But while in school, I found that I really enjoyed being in the pediatric ward. It was where I felt most energized. I really feel like I see the most immediate good working with kids. Does that make sense?"

"Absolutely," he said, sipping his coffee. "It's almost exactly how I got into it myself. The instant gratification of helping a young person, who you know will most certainly live a better and much longer life because of your help... it is incredible. Don't get me wrong, I enjoy my other work too. Anything I can do here in Monroe, I do, and for anyone that needs it. But there is a special feeling I get from helping children. I know they will almost all outlive me. But they will be able to because I helped them at some point. It's sort of selfish, but it's gratifying."

"Agreed," I said, downing my cup.

"Well, looks like time we ought to get back," Dr. Jones

said. Like magic, the intercom system popped on and one of the ladies from the nurses' desk called for him.

"How did you do that?" I asked.

"Magic," he said.

Fourteen hours on my feet and I was finally clocking out. I had to be back in soon enough and essentially had enough time to stop by a sandwich shop, grab something to eat, then bring it home and shovel it in before bed. Not that I particularly felt capable of doing anything else anyway.

I was bone-tired, but fulfilled. I hadn't run into anyone I knew yet, so I was calling that a win so far. The operative phrase was "so far," since Monroe was only but so big. I was bound to see people I went to school with or knew from around town coming in with their kids or wives or husbands. It was going to happen eventually. I just had to be prepared for it.

Dr. Jones had been very effusive about me, which made me feel great. Several times in the day he asked me to do something first-year residents didn't often get to do. He treated me less like a resident and more like a fellow pediatrician, though clearly one who was below him on the pecking order. His word was final, and the few times he corrected me, he framed it in front of patients as competing theories but that the official stance of the hospital was his.

When I did something well, Dr. Jones was quick to point it out. It was silly I could be swayed by such basic reward behavioral tactics, but I couldn't deny it was working. I respected Dr. Jones and wanted him to respect me too. This meant being my absolute best and making sure I didn't screw up anything. And, as Dr. Jones pointed out before I left, punctuality was everything.

The day had moved in a blur, but now I was on my way home. After fourteen hours on my feet, and a warm pizza in my hand, I was ready to get inside and crash. Thinking I would eat, shower, and then sleep, I let myself relax on the couch with the pizza. It was a huge mistake. I woke up at two in the morning, a cold slice of pizza resting half-eaten on my chest and the television blaring. The shower would have to wait for the morning.

CHAPTER 6

CARRIE

My alarm went off Wednesday morning just like it was supposed to, and I got out of bed to start my day on my normal schedule. It seemed the strangeness of the day before had just been a hiccup.

By the time I got out of the shower and was doing my makeup with plenty of time in my morning routine to spare, I was feeling like the discomfort of the day before was far behind me. Everything was back to normal, and my weird thoughts about bad omens and negativity that might be lurking around every corner ready to strike were gone from my mind.

I was the one who got to wake Amelia up just like usual. I gave her breakfast, and we walked out of the house with lunches in hand and supper ready to be cooked when we got home. It was going to be a good day, I told myself. A good, predictable day.

It wouldn't take long for me to be proven wrong.

When I got to the bakery, Parker was pulling a tray of fresh cinnamon rolls out of one of the massive ovens. It instantly filled the space with the warm, rich smell of butter, sugar, and cinnamon. This was one of those smells I could happily breathe in all day, every day and never get tired of it

, which was a good thing considering we baked them every day, year round.

The cinnamon rolls were a big seller, especially during the colder months of the year. Once the holiday season hit, they outsold just about everything, and I ended up trimming my menu down by a few items just to accommodate the rolls.

I drew in a deep lungful of the scent and smiled at Parker. "They smell amazing."

"Of course they do," he said, laughing as he moved the tray to one of the large cooling racks. "You made them. I'm responsible for oven transport only."

"But you do round trip," I pointed out. "That's very important."

"True," he acquiesced.

I grabbed one of the aprons and tied it around my waist as I pushed through the doors into the front of the bakery. Maggie stood behind the counter, waiting patiently while a customer perused the muffins with the seriousness of selecting their next home. I flashed a smile at the line forming behind her and lifted my eyebrows a bit.

"Can I help you?" I asked.

The next customer slipped out of the line and came to me. I made her a coffee and tucked the two Danishes and a croissant she wanted into a bag before wishing her a good day and calling the next. By the time I was finished with the third customer, Maggie had packed up three flavors of muffins, but the customer was still deep in contemplation about more.

I called up the next customer and smiled widely when I saw it was one of my mother's oldest friends.

"Good morning, Mrs. Cramer," I said. "How are you doing today?"

"Good morning, Carrie," she said. "Can you believe the weather we've been having?"

There was nothing particularly spectacular about the weather. This was just her signature opening for pretty much any conversation. It had been for as long as I could remember. No matter what the situation or where we ran into her, more often than not, the tiny woman would start the conversation by marveling at the weather.

The line had lessened a little bit, and Maggie had finally moved on to another customer, so I didn't feel too bad taking some time to chat with Mrs. Cramer. She got the same order every time she came in, so I hung out there by the counter with her for a few moments before putting together what she wanted. We caught up with each other and sent our greetings to each other's families before saying goodbye.

I had just tucked the tip money she always insisted on giving me into the jar on the counter and bent down to get a few more treats to put in the display case when the door chimed to indicate more people coming in. I glanced up at Maggie, but she was juggling a large office order.

"Just one second," I called up from behind the case. "I'll be right with you."

"Take your time."

The voice made my heart jump. I knew it almost as well as my own even though it had been years since I'd heard it. Getting to my feet, I looked over the counter, and my breath caught in my chest.

"Travis," I managed to force through my throat.

His eyes locked with mine, and it felt like we were stuck in that moment. I was fairly certain I heard him mutter a swear word under his breath, and I bristled, not able to figure out what he was thinking or what that reaction was supposed to mean.

I refused to show any emotion. Instead, I just stood tall, my shoulders down and my head up, looking right at him. Everyone's eyes were on us. They heard me say his name and probably heard him muttering too. I didn't want to become a spectacle. At least Mrs. Cramer wasn't there anymore.

We were two adults, and we were standing in a bakery. There was a standard transaction right there, ready to happen between us. It didn't even require a lot of thought. I just needed to keep my confidence and control and move through it with as much speed and dignity as I could manage.

In front of me, Travis seemed to have the same moment of realization, then the same talking-to with himself. He straightened up and gave a tiny wiggle. The gesture was imperceptible, and most people around him probably didn't even notice it happen. But I did. I'd seen it countless times before. It was something he did when he was trying to shake something off and get his thoughts back under his control.

He seemed to get over the shock and walked up to the counter so we were only a couple of feet apart. It was the closest we had been to each other in seven years.

I wasn't sure what to do or say. The whole set transaction I was relying on went right out of my head. I might have been able to fake that I was feeling confident and look perfectly calm and collected, but this situation was something I wasn't at all prepared to handle.

I didn't know how long we were standing there just

staring at each other and feeling awkward before Parker came out of the kitchen. Out of the corner of my eye, I saw him pause and look back and forth between Travis and me. When he realized neither of us was moving, he stepped up beside me.

"Good morning. What can I get for you?" he asked.

I stepped back, happy to let my staff handle it.

The room felt like it was closing in on me. Suddenly, I was having trouble breathing and my head was spinning. Still striving not to show it, I walked through the double doors leading into the kitchen and tried to drag in a breath. It wouldn't seem to go into my lungs. They were heavy and aching in my chest. My heart started pounding, and it felt like I had just run around the block a few times at full speed.

I stood close to the doors, waiting for Maggie or Parker to come back there. At any moment, I was expecting one of them to come back and tell me Travis wanted me to come out and talk with him. But they never did.

Carefully approaching the door, I pushed it open just enough to glance into the front of the bakery and look around. Travis was gone.

That was supposed to make me feel better. Instead, it only made it harder to breathe. I rushed into my office and shut the door behind me. Sitting down hard in my chair, I kept trying to suck in a breath. I reached for my phone and called my mother.

"Hey, honey," she said.

"Mom."

"What is it? What's wrong?" she asked, her voice changing from the casual greeting to concerned and on edge.

"I think I'm having a panic attack."

"Why? What happened? Where are you?"

"I'm at work," I said.

"Are you hurt?" she asked.

Leave it to a mother to be so worried about her child that she doesn't give enough room in the conversation to actually find out what's going on. I shook my head even though I knew she couldn't see me and fought to calm down enough to speak.

"No. Travis came in."

There was silence on the other end of the line for several seconds.

"Travis?" she finally asked. "He came into the bakery?"

"Yes. He just walked right in," I said.

"Was he looking for you?" She was obviously uncomfortable with even considering that idea.

"No. He seemed just as shocked to see me as I was to see him. And not happy. Parker waited on him for me, and then he left."

Talking about it sent me into another round of gasping for breath.

"Calm down," Mom said. "Just try to relax and breathe. The fact that he didn't want to talk is a blessing. He got out, and you didn't have to interact with him. That's a good thing, right?"

"I guess," I said.

The truth was the prospect of a conversation with him was terrifying.

"Alright, so what now? What should we do?" she asked.

I knew exactly what she was asking. It was a question she'd asked me a little less than seven years ago, and it was even more relevant now. So, I gave her the same answer I gave her then.

"We don't say anything."

41

"You're sure?" she asked.

I knew it was wrong. There wasn't any way to creatively word or present it so that it wasn't. But that didn't change my decision. I was going to continue to keep my secret. I'd been doing it for years. I didn't see any reason to change now.

CHAPTER 7

TRAVIS

Clammy skin. Hyperventilation. Nausea. Rapid heartbeat.

It was all there. I was in shock. These weren't the words of a dramatic person who threw around medical terminology without knowing what they were talking about because they thought it sounded good. I knew the signs. I recognized them from my training.

The utter surprise I'd just faced was the emotional equivalent of running at full force into a brick wall, and it left me struggling to react. I held the box of pastries with an iron grip and nearly spilled the coffee on me as I backed out of the door, my eyes washing over the spot Carrie had been standing one last time. I barely heard myself speak—my voice came as if I was under miles of seawater, and the boat of sanity was far, far above me.

Walking back outside was not unlike suddenly finding myself awake in a dream. The world seemed to expand and contract with my own breath, and my knees felt weak under me. Somehow, someway, I made it to the hospital. I had no idea how. Muscle memory and the familiarity of the area was enough to get me there without the proper intervention of coherent thought. The parking lot was mostly empty as I made my way through it in a haze of emotion and thought. I was completely lost inside my own mind and walking in, I was glad to see I had still made it there just before Dr. Jones.

I meandered to the back and sat the goodies on the table in the breakroom. I stood there, staring blankly at the hallway until Dr. Jones rounded the corner while checking his watch. He was still a few minutes early, but I had made it there before him again. Punctuality was important to him, and despite being shaken to my core, I still managed to pull it off. How effective I would be otherwise was still up in the air.

Dr. Jones made his way to the nurses' desk first, saying good morning and checking for any messages. Ari, one of the nurses, handed him a slip of paper with a handwritten note which he nodded at and asked to be put in the patient's file. Then he turned and walked into the breakroom, an amiable smile on his face.

"Good morning, Travis," he said. He seemed to be in a good mood, perhaps even better than usual as he eyed the table in the center of the room.

"I got these," I said lamely, indicating the box of pastries and carrier with coffee for him. "The black coffee is the one with B written on the side."

"Oh, you got jelly filled. My favorite," he said, picking up one of the pastries. He seemed genuinely delighted. "Come with me." We walked along the hall until we reached a door that had the doctor's name emblazoned on the nameplate on the side. "Take a seat," he said, sitting at his desk, shaking his mouse to wake the computer up and stuffing the rest of the pastry into his mouth.

I sat hard in the chair in the cramped office. Papers were literally everywhere, stuffed in manilla envelopes and clear folders and stacked on tables and chairs. For all the sanctimony about being early, Dr. Jones seemed to have no such hang-ups about staying organized. His office was a wreck, but at least it had a comfortable chair. I leaned back and held my coffee tight to my chest. The warmth against my skin seemed to bring me out of my fog a bit, as did the smell of the dark roast.

But I was still gone. Lost in the mind that was reeling from seeing Carrie in the pastry shop. She was still gorgeous—that was the first thing I'd noticed. The time had only done wonderful things for her, and she was every bit as captivating as she had been when we were young, but now she had the advantage of maturity. She was so damned stunning that even if I had the ability to speak to her despite the awkwardness of our history, I was pretty sure her beauty would have left me stammering anyway.

It was shock. Real, clinical, complete shock. I knew it. It still gripped my heart.

I had to get it out of my head, though. Dr. Jones was talking, and I knew I had missed some of what he was saying. Seeming groggy or aloof was the last thing I needed, so I had to just pretend I had been following along and catch as much of what he was yammering about as I could.

"So," he said, continuing some line of thought I completely missed, "I think that a steady diet of high protein should do the trick for the muscle atrophy, but I'll be damned if I know what to do about her sweating attacks."

"Yoga," I muttered, then realized I had spoken. Dr. Jones turned to me; his eyes scrunched up in confusion. I was about to kick myself for not having enough control not

45

to speak when his eyebrows rose, and a smile stretched across his face.

"You know what," he said, "that might actually help. She's a bit young, but her attacks might be tied to anxiety, and yoga could be a good physical activity. Good idea."

I smiled weakly. "I've heard it works wonders."

Happily, Dr. Jones wrote some notes down and excused himself before making his way back with a number of charts and forms. The day's schedule was already booked solid, and we still had to be ready as backup for emergency as well. It was going to be a long day, and I needed to keep my focus so the doc didn't notice anything was amiss. If he had already, he hadn't said anything or made any indication one way or the other.

I made my way into the breakroom and grabbed a pastry and wolfed it down. The sugar hit was almost instantaneous, and it helped clear my mind a bit more. I wished I could say the same thing for the coffee. Trying to copy the good doctor and slide my way into less complicated coffee resulted in an unpleasant experience akin to drinking boiled dirt. Still, I forced it down as quickly as I could and refilled the cup with something a little less black and a little milkier.

As the day began, I felt pretty okay, but as morning wore on into afternoon, the slog got worse, and charts and patients began to blur. I found myself seeming to mentally doze off, my mind wandering back to Carrie. Carrie and how beautiful she looked. Carrie and how shocked she looked. Carrie and how sad she looked.

Carrie, and how she was only a few miles away from me, standing behind the counter of a pastry shop, living her life without me. Knowing that it was no one's fault but my own. I owned that.

Lunch couldn't come fast enough, and I zipped out of

the building to take it outside. I took a walk to the cafeteria, going the long way outside rather than walking through the halls, and grabbed a sandwich that I ate at a bench in the grass. I had an hour of break, making up for how few breaks I got during the course of the day, and I thought very seriously of finding a place to take a nap. Maybe that would clear my head.

Having wolfed down the sandwich, I figured there wasn't much to lose by trying. The breakroom had an attached overnight room for nurses and doctors stuck there who needed a rest. It had three bunk beds but no windows. The darkness was soothing, and I felt a little bit of the tension slide away when I lay down on one of the mattresses. Setting an alarm for twenty minutes, I closed my eyes.

Sleep didn't come. Instead, I tossed and turned, always finding something wrong with the position or simply letting my thoughts get too frustrating until I forced myself to flip over and think about something else. Twenty infuriating minutes later and I felt just as spacey and tired as I had already.

When the alarm went off, I sat up and rubbed my face with my palms. Yawning, I stood and put my sneakers back on. The darkness was beckoning me to lie back down, but I knew that even if I had all the time in the world left on my break, sleep wouldn't come. Not yet.

I got back to work and tried not to let my mind wander but caught myself more than once stumbling over my words or writing the wrong thing down and needing to erase it. I was wildly unlike my normal self, and it bugged me that I couldn't get my mind straight. Even if I wasn't actively thinking about Carrie and the run-in we'd had, I just couldn't get into the groove. When my shift was over and the new attendings had taken their spots on the rounds, I clocked out and headed for the door.

Dr. Jones was standing there by the door to the parking lot, his jacket folded over his arm and another pastry in his hand.

"Travis, can I speak to you for a moment while we walk to my car?" he asked. It was less of a question and more him informing me that we were doing so. I nodded and we walked outside.

"I just wanted to address your performance today," he said. "You seemed to be rather distracted. Not at all like what I've seen from you so far."

I nodded. "Yeah, I feel like—" I began, but he cut me off.

"It doesn't matter what it was," he said. "Whatever it is, you leave it outside the doors. People inside that building deserve the best from us. The absolute best. Their lives might depend on it. I am sure you understand that."

He wasn't rude or demeaning in his manner, but there was a curtness to his words. I nodded again, and he responded with one of his own as he opened the door to his car.

"Yes, sir," I said.

"Very well," he said, sitting in the driver's seat. "Good evening, Dr. King."

With that, he shut the door and drove away.

He was absolutely right about the people in there deserving the best care they could get, and that was precisely why I couldn't stay. There was too much of my past in this place. Too many of my own hang-ups, my own stressors. Too many people who expected me to fail, and to fail so miserably that I would fulfill the destiny laid out for me by my parents.

The next three years would be torture if I stayed. Absolute and complete mental and physical torture. Being this close to Carrie and being reminded every day of what I did to her when I left, being in the town where everyone expected me to screw up like my family did and being under the watchful eye of a very attentive and stern doctor was too much. Maybe I could put in for a transfer. Somewhere far away from the stress and expectations.

Somewhere far away from Carrie.

CHAPTER 8

CARRIE

Thursday morning started smoothly like Wednesday had. At least, it did if I was only thinking about my schedule. My alarm went off, and I got out of bed. I took my shower and got dressed. I made breakfast and packed lunches. Everything was going just the way it was supposed to. But it felt far from smooth.

As I went through the motions of my morning, I couldn't get the image of Travis's face out of my mind. The image of his face lingered as I drove Amelia to school and got stronger when she leaned forward to kiss me goodbye and slid from the back seat to run over to her little cluster of friends.

Watching her made my heart tighten. I saw the features she shared with her father every time I looked at her, but I tried not to let myself think about it. I tried not to let myself see his eyes or the little crinkles beside them when she smiled at me. I tried not to let myself see the facial expressions she made that I saw countless times, or the way she slept that looked just like him.

Just like I had from the day she was born, I tried to see

only her when I looked at Amelia. She was just my daughter, and I didn't want to notice the pieces of him in her. But now I couldn't avoid them. Seeing him again had only highlighted those features, and now as I watched her go into the school, they stood out strongly.

It left me feeling a little out of sorts and shaky as I made my way to the bakery. Maybe it was naive of me to think I would never encounter Travis again. It was a coping mechanism, a survival technique in a way. I could tell myself that he just wasn't a part of my existence anymore and let myself move forward.

Of course, there were days when that was easier said than done. I couldn't just completely cut his existence out of my awareness. After all, he was a huge part of my life. He became an even bigger part when I found out I was pregnant. Amelia existing meant I couldn't just compartmentalize him in the back of my mind and pretend he had never been.

But that didn't mean I was ready to see him again. It didn't mean I wanted to come face-to-face with him, especially when I wasn't prepared. I came to terms with the reality that I would raise my daughter as a single mother a long time ago. The decision not to find and tell Travis about the baby happened during my pregnancy, and I'd never wavered on it.

Now suddenly I felt like I had to rethink it. Seeing him took him out of the abstract and put him very firmly back into my reality. It brought up questions and thoughts I didn't expect to have but couldn't push out of my mind.

It seemed I wasn't the only one who was still thinking about the encounter with Travis. I had only been in the bakery for half an hour when I looked up and saw my parents standing outside on the sidewalk, looking at me through the glass front of the shop.

I waved and gestured for them to come in. They walked in, and I smiled.

"Hey," I said. "This is a surprise. Can I get you something?"

"Actually, honey, we wanted to talk to you for a minute," Mom said. "Are you busy? Is this a good time?"

The morning crowd had been fairly light, and when I looked over at Maggie and Parker, they nodded to confirm they could handle the customers.

"Sure," I said. "Come on back to the office."

I made coffee and put the cups in a carrier, then filled a plate with pastries and breads from the display case.

We walked into the back of the bakery, and I closed the office door behind us. My parents sat on the couch, and I put the coffee and plate in front of them, taking my cup before sitting in the chair positioned to the side of them.

"So, I heard you saw Travis yesterday," my father said to start the conversation.

I could already tell this probably wasn't going to go well. Whenever he started a conversation in that falsely-casual way, I knew it was going to go downhill rapidly. I took a sip of my coffee and reached for one of the croissants on the plate.

"Yes. He came in here. But I went back in the kitchen almost as soon as he walked in, so we didn't interact or anything," I said.

"That's good. I wouldn't want to think you would let him get to you again," he said.

And there it was. We got to the judgment part even faster than I thought.

"What do you mean by that?"

He reached for one of the remaining cups of coffee and glanced down into it like he didn't completely trust a cup I made for him. I was already regretting going to the effort.

"I just mean you don't have the best track record when it comes to decisions that have to do with that boy. I'm glad to hear you didn't let seeing him distract you from the life you've built for yourself and ruin anything," he said as if it made everything better.

"He's hardly a boy anymore, Dad. And I don't understand what you mean by me letting him distract me," I said, even though I was fairly certain I did know what he was talking about.

"We're just concerned you might start having thoughts about him and be tempted to make certain disclosures in hopes of reconnecting," Mom said.

This was just getting more awkward and offensive the longer it went on. I didn't necessarily think it was going to be as smooth and supportive as my mother talking me down from my panic attack the day before, but I also wasn't prepared for it to go this sideways this fast.

"Is that your way of saying you think I would tell him about Amelia hoping to what? Trap him into staying this time?" I asked.

"Well," Mom said, shrugging slightly and looking over at my father.

"That's exactly what we're worried about," he said.

I didn't know which one of them I was more upset with in that moment.

"You two do remember that whether or not I involved Travis in Amelia's life was and continues to be my decision, and only mine," I said firmly.

"We're not saying it isn't your decision," my father said. "But I don't want you to lose sight of everything you've been through. And everything we've helped you through. You made the choice not to include him from the very beginning, and I don't want you to go back on that just because he's suddenly right in front of you again and it's tempting."

"You act like I'm some lovesick idiot who can't make my own decisions."

"That's not it—" Mom started.

"But here's the thing," I said, brushing past whatever it was that she was planning on saying. "Maybe it isn't so simple to make that decision anymore. It was easier when I first decided not to tell him because he had just left. He walked out on me, and I hadn't been able to get in touch with him. I figured it was just easier that way. But now..."

"Now?" Dad asked, his voice lifting slightly like he couldn't believe I actually sounded like I might not agree completely with the decision anymore.

"Now I've seen him again, and it isn't as easy to just push aside anymore. A big part of me is really tired of hiding Amelia and thinks Travis has a right to know about her. And that she has a right to know him as well. He is her father." I stuffed a bite of the croissant into my mouth and let out a sigh, thinking for a few moments before speaking again. "But another part of me is still so pissed off that he left me the way he did."

"Exactly. He left you. Without any explanation or any consideration to you or how you felt. Is that really the kind of man you want to share your child with? Can you imagine the complication and frustration it could cause? What if he acted like he wanted to be a part of her life and was interested in getting to know her better, then just disappeared again? Think about how hard that would be for you, but also for Amelia," Dad said.

"Well he didn't really leave of his own volition, did he?"

I leveled my gaze at my father who at least had the decency to avert his eyes.

"She's already almost seven years old," Mom jumped in. "She is aware that she doesn't have a father the way the other children do. But she's also accustomed to it. This is her life and the only one she's ever known. Introducing him into it could be extremely disruptive."

"Look," Dad said. "You've worked so hard to build the life you have for yourself and for her. I wouldn't think you would want to risk that for him."

"I don't," I agreed.

He nodded. "Then you need to protect it. You need to keep everything the way it is."

"Alright," I said. "We'll keep it the way it is. For now."

My parents nodded back at me.

"Good," Mom said. "You're making the right decision. Now, I don't think Amelia should come here after school."

"Why?"

"If he came here once, he could come again. It would be better if he didn't run into her by accident. For the next few days, she should stay home after school."

"You're right," I said, feeling a twinge at the thought. I really enjoyed having my daughter at the bakery with me, but I knew that would be a bad situation. It also brought up another thought. "I guess that means she shouldn't come during the holiday baking either."

Usually during a holiday season when we were doing specialty products Amelia would come with me to the bakery and she stayed through the day. It was a fun time for us to spend together, and she enjoyed being around the baking and the customers. But now I worried if she was there, Travis would come in and see her.

I couldn't risk that. Even though it was possible, and

even probable, Travis wouldn't stop in again, I needed that extra layer of security. There were just too many variables, and I wasn't sure how to keep them all going. If he did see her and started asking questions, I didn't know if I would be able to maintain the lie right to his face. It was just easier to keep them totally separated.

For the rest of the week, I was on alert. Every time the door chimed, my eyes snapped up, expecting it to be him walking in. I was constantly waiting for him to come back in or to be waiting for me when I walked into the front of the bakery from the kitchen. But he didn't come.

By Sunday, the stress and anxiety had gotten to me. I was so exhausted. I felt like I could barely keep my head up. It was the one day of the week I kept the bakery closed, so I was home with Amelia. I packed her up and headed to my parents' house so she could play with her grandparents and get more attention than I felt physically capable of giving.

I barely made it to the couch before falling asleep.

CHAPTER 9

TRAVIS

Tuesday was terrible. Not just for the shock of seeing Carrie, but for how I went through the day completely acting like a man without functioning brain cells. I made an idiot of myself in front of a man I truly respected and went home in an emotional and mental fog. I didn't even bother with eating dinner. Instead I opted towards taking a shower, nearly inhaling a protein bar, brushing my teeth, and going to bed. A full night's sleep had me feeling a little bit better and avoiding the bakery for the rest of the week allowed me to get back to some sort of normalcy.

I swore I would never act like I had again. I could keep her out of my mind and focus on the job. I knew I could. I had to when I got sober and went back to school, so I knew I could do it again. I had to do it. Not just for me, but to prove to everyone in Monroe that they were wrong about me. I wasn't a screw-up. I was good at my chosen profession, and if I could get my brain straight, I could help the town and help myself.

Then, eventually, I'd get the hell out of Monroe for

good and never, ever look back. That thought by itself was worth pressuring myself to not let something as silly as emotion ruin my abilities. I just had to lean into that and focus on what I was capable of. Knowing how much good I could do was the unknown and the exciting. Eyes on the prize.

Then, Saturday morning came.

I was shocked I had the day off. I walked in on Friday, fulling expecting the next week's schedule to begin with a weekend of me at the hospital, but Dr. Jones had personally noted that he wanted me to have Saturday off. When I asked him why, he simply smiled and said I had picked myself back up and deserved a little time to myself.

"We've been working you a bit harder than we usually put our residents through," Dr. Jones said.

"Well, I'm not going to say no to more sleep," I laughed.

"I would expect not," he said and clapped my shoulder before heading back into his rounds. Because of the good news, Friday seemed to fly by.

When I finally clocked out, I made it home and spoiled myself with an evening of pasta and bad television late into the night before crashing. Waking up near noon, I was feeling almost myself again. The pasta had represented the first meal I'd made myself in the new place, though it also represented the extent of my groceries. I was going to have to head to the store so I could pick up a few things and not have to rely entirely on the cafeteria and delivery. The upside of saving money while working there wasn't really coming to fruition if I spent everything on food being delivered.

There were a few grocery stores in town, but the one I went to was one I had a good feeling Carrie wouldn't possibly be at. It was a newer place and just at the edge of town. Carrie and her family were always loyal to a few specific places, and if I avoided going to them, I had a decent chance of avoiding her. I hated that she dictated my movements, but it was better than seeing her again and throwing myself off my game again.

As I pulled into the grocery store, I noticed a truck that looked vaguely familiar outside. It wasn't so much the model of the truck, but the stickers that adorned it. Several crude drawings of cartoon characters doing things very unlike their authorized images and loyalty stickers to various brands adorned the back. Somewhere in my brain I knew who drove that truck, but I couldn't place it right off. The question was answered almost immediately, however, when I walked in and came face-to-face with Hank Huber.

At six foot six, Hank was a tall, skinny, wild-looking man. A dark brown beard stretched to the center of his chest, and he often had it in braids. Today it was tied at the end with tiny rubber bands in neon colors. His wild, bushy eyebrows were raised in surprise when he saw me, and his arms went out to the side for a massive bear hug. I had no choice but to lean in, since his reach was so damn long, he was going to catch me anyway.

"Travis King?" he said in his surprisingly high-pitched voice. "Is that really you?"

"It is," I said, extricating myself from his grip. "How are you, Hank?"

"Oh, you know me," Hank said, tucking his thumbs into his jeans. "Can't complain, though I will try. How about you? I haven't seen you around these parts in, what, like three or four years?"

"It's been a while," I said, brushing my hand through my hair. I just wanted to go grab a few ingredients and get out of there. But Hank wasn't going to let me off that easy.

"Shame about your folks, huh?" he said. His eyes were filled with sadness, and I tried to screw up my face to make it seem like I agreed with him. "Your dad was the coolest guy. My goodness do I miss him," he said. "Course, your mom was alright too, you know. Fine woman. Just a shame."

I nodded in agreement. Though I didn't really agree. Hank had been a family friend for as far back as I could remember. Dad had described him as his best friend, and I was sure the feeling was mutual. When I was little, Hank was a constant presence at our place, or us at his place. I didn't mind it so much as while Hank liked to drink, but he wasn't a partier. He and Dad would go out on the porch on summer days and put away a twenty-four-pack, sure, but they weren't going to go anywhere and do anything worse than that. No fights at bars, no carousing, no disappearing for days at a time. If Dad was drinking with Hank, he'd be safe and likely sleep it off on his couch.

"I hate to do this, Hank, but I am awful starved, and I need to grab some stuff to take home to cook," I said.

"You hungry?" A lightbulb seeming to go off above his head. I could just imagine it. One with the pull strings for sure.

"I am. I was just coming by to grab a few things for my place."

"Well, hell, why don't you come out to the diner with me?" Hank asked. There was so much hope in his voice that I didn't immediately say no. It seemed to be all he needed. He elbowed my arm and laughed. "Of course, come on, Travis. We can catch up. You can do boring old shopping later. Let's go. My treat."

I couldn't find it in me to turn him down. He had always been good to me and he was offering to pay for my lunch. What else was I going to do? I followed him out to his truck, which he proudly displayed to me.

"Still running," he said. "Come on, hop in. I'll bring you right back here when we're done."

Against my better judgment, I got in the passenger's seat and rode with Hank a few blocks down to the diner. He began talking on the drive about the truck and how much work he had put into it to keep it going, but I wasn't paying much attention. The truck itself seemed like it was going to fall apart any second.

The diner was one of those greasy spoons I almost never stopped in, but when I did, I realized I loved it. It was no different there, and when we got a booth, I chowed down the fries they brought to us as a perfunctory thing, like how Italian places would bring bread service.

"You remember when your dad would bring you here with us?" Hank asked. "He loved this place almost as much as he loved anything else in the world. He'd eat this sandwich they have—they call it the Monster. You should order it."

"No, that's alright."

"No, no, you should," Hank insisted. "You would love it. It'd be just like hanging out with your old man."

"No, it wouldn't," I said, rather sternly. Hank looked crestfallen for a moment. "Sorry. I've just been running pretty ragged at work, you know? And Dad and I didn't get along at the end there, and all of that is just... complicated."

Technically, it was the truth. It was complicated. I didn't know exactly how I felt about being alone without my parents even on the Earth, but I knew that it had thus far been better than when they were here and drunk or drugged out. That I knew for sure.

"That's fine," Hank said, picking up his menu and

examining it, presumably so he didn't have to look me in the face. "Everybody deals with it their own way."

I was half-tempted to tell him I had dealt with it already and avoiding talking about him was one way of doing so. Instead, I picked up my menu too. "How is the Caesar salad?" I asked.

Hank looked at me over the top of the menu for a moment before snorting derisively. "Salad," he muttered. "Like I eat salad."

The conversation dipped after that until the orders were taken, and Hank asked where I had been and what I had been up to—and why I had chosen to stay away.

"I just was busy. School was hard and took up most of my time. After my parents died, there didn't seem to be any reason to come back."

Hank nodded, digging into his food. He seemed upset.

"I get that, but what about the house?"

"I haven't stepped foot into that place since they passed," I said. "Don't intend to either. It was their place, not mine."

"I disagree," Hank said. "I know you have your issues with your folks, but that place is your legacy. It's what they left you."

"All my folks left me was trouble. Trouble and bills and a bad name."

"Your father was a hell of a man," Hank began, anger starting to rise in his face.

"No, he wasn't," I said, cutting him off. "He was a drunk and an addict and an awful father. You might have liked him, but you didn't know him when he was alone with us. Alone with me." I reached into my wallet and pulled out a twenty-dollar bill. "I think I'm done. This should cover my portion. I don't want to owe anyone anything. Especially not because of their relationship with my father."

I stormed off. I knew I was probably being a bit irrational, but I couldn't help it. Hank defending my father was just too much. It brought up too much. I walked the several blocks back to the grocery store stewing about it, and when I got there, I forewent the groceries and got in the car. On my way home, at a stoplight, I looked to my left and saw the liquor store.

Licking my lips, my thoughts turned to the taste of sweet whiskey. How it would burn so good in my chest on the way down. How just a little bit of time and money and I could wipe all this Dad shit out of my mind.

A horn behind me alerted me that the light was green, and I punched the gas pedal. I went home and immediately went inside to my room, pulling up my phone. The number I dialed was one I had memorized by heart, a rarity. My sponsor picked up on the second ring.

CHAPTER 10

CARRIE

I woke up in the middle of Sunday afternoon to the smell of my mother's cooking still lingering in the air. She had made meatballs for lunch, and I could only hope there was a big bowl waiting for me on the kitchen counter.

Groaning slightly as I sat up, I stretched my neck to loosen up the muscles made tense by sleeping on the couch. When it felt like I got all the kinks out and could move, I stood and made my way across the living room toward the kitchen. I could hear voices talking and laughing, and when I stepped into the room, I found my mother and daughter wearing matching aprons as they rolled out cookies on the kitchen island.

There was another of those aprons in one of the kitchen drawers with my name embroidered in script across the front just like my mother's and Amelia's. Mom had ordered them for us the year before to commemorate our annual Christmas cookie baking sessions. I knew how excited both of them were to get the aprons out again, and now that Valentine's Day was coming up, it seemed they couldn't wait a second longer.

"Making cookies already?" I asked, stepping up to the side of the island to check out their progress.

"We are considering it a practice session," Mom said.

"Our real baking session is next week," Amelia said. "I want to make perfect hearts."

I smiled and ran my hand over her hair before leaning down to kiss the top of her head. "Then you should definitely practice. I will just have to make the sacrifice of eating up your practice cookies."

"Grampa, too," Amelia said. "I promised him."

I laughed. "Well, of course, Grampa too." I snagged one of the bits of cookie dough that fell from the side of one of the cookie cutters and popped it into my mouth before my mother could tell me not to.

"Are there any meatballs left?"

"They're on the stove," my mother said.

I got a bowl down from the cabinet and used the ladle on the spoon rest beside the pot to fish out several of the meatballs along with some of the rich red sauce they were swimming in. A sprinkle of cheese finished the dish, and I reached into the flatware drawer to get out a fork so I could dive into it.

The oven timer went off just as I was taking my first bite, and I stepped aside to let Mom grab potholders and open the door. She pulled out a fresh sheet of cookies, which explained the hint of sweetness I smelled under the savory meatballs when I woke up.

"I'm going to bring these into the dining room to cool," Mom announced. "Carrie, will you grab a cooling rack and help me? Amelia, sweetie, just keep rolling, and when you're done, cut out the cookies so we can start the next batch."

Mom nodded her head to the side to gesture for me to

follow her. The expression on her face told me that there was more to this a little trip through the house than just putting the cookies somewhere to cool out of the way.

I reached into one of the lower cabinets and pulled out a cooling rack. Carrying it in one hand and my bowl of meatballs in the other, I followed my mother to the dining room. I set the cooling rack down, and she placed the cookie sheet onto it. Rather than heading back to the kitchen, Mom sat down.

I followed her lead, sitting down and taking another bite of my food.

"Everything okay?" I asked.

"I just wanted a chance to talk to you without Amelia hearing. You need to know why you saw Travis at the bakery," she said.

My heart sank a little bit. "What do you mean?"

"He wasn't just visiting or driving through town. I heard through the grapevine that he is at the local hospital doing his residency."

I was shocked. "I didn't know he finished his undergraduate degree, much less medical school."

Mom nodded. "Apparently he did quite well. Now he's here doing his residency in pediatrics."

This surprised me even more. Of course, I knew Travis had wanted to be a doctor. But he had never mentioned that particular specialty when he first went into the pre-med program. Something about him specifically studying to work with children made my heart squeeze. Then a realization came to me.

"He's doing his residency here?" I asked.

"Yes. At Monroe General."

"That means he's going to be here for three years. At the

very least. He could get a job here after his residency ends," I said.

"That's true. That's why I wanted to talk to you about it."

I stared down into my bowl of meatballs, wondering how the hell I was supposed to go about avoiding Travis for three whole years at the absolute minimum. It was stressful enough just thinking about running into him again for one week. It was going to completely push me over the edge if I had to try to keep up with my secret for that long.

I just had to take one day at a time.

It was what was still on my mind the next morning when my alarm went off. Amelia didn't have school that day due to a teacher in-service but was already up when I got out of the shower.

While I made breakfast, she sat at the table with paper and her crayons spread out around her. Out of the corner of my eye, I saw she was drawing an elaborate and lacy heart. She was obviously excited about Valentine's Day. I, on the other hand, was not.

I hadn't had much of a romantic life since Amelia had been born. I'd gone on a few dates here and there, but raising a daughter and opening my own business didn't leave a whole lot of room for love. And now that the one man I had ever loved was back in town for the foreseeable future, well that dampened my holiday spirit even more. As far as I was concerned, that fat little bastard Cupid could shoot his arrow elsewhere. "Honey, do you want to come to the bakery with me today?" I asked as I made breakfast.

She looked over her shoulder at me. "I thought I was going to Grandma's house."

"You can. But I just wanted to see if you might want to come with me instead."

Her face lit up, and she shook her head. "I want to be with you."

I picked up the phone and called my mother to let her know I wouldn't be bringing Amelia over that morning. It was very obvious my mother didn't agree with that decision, but I wouldn't let her talk me out of it. I got off the phone just as my coffee maker was finished brewing my first cup. Leaving the breakfast to finish cooking, I went over and looked down at Amelia's drawing again.

"That's a very pretty heart," I told her.

"It's for Aiden," she said with a giggle in her voice.

Oh boy. I wasn't ready for this. "Aiden, eh?"

"Yeah, he's cute." Another giggle.

"Well anyone would be lucky for you to draw them such a beautiful Valentine," I told her.

Amelia got quiet for a moment and looked pensive.

"What's up kiddo?" I asked her.

"Was my daddy your Valentine?" she asked.

I nearly choked on my coffee, but she just smiled at me and went back to drawing.

An hour later, we arrived at the bakery. While Amelia was hanging up her coat and putting her bag of books, coloring supplies, and toys in the office for when she needed a break, I went to talk to Maggie and Parker.

"Do you guys remember that man who came in last week and we just kind of stared at each other?" I asked.

I wished there was a more subtle and less embarrassing way to ask that question, but there really wasn't. Both of them nodded.

"Yeah, I had to help him because you weren't," Parker said.

"That's the one. I need you to keep an eye out for him," I said.

"Why?" Maggie asked.

"I just do. If you see him, just let me know."

They agreed a moment before Amelia came out of the kitchen into the front of the bakery. They both gushed over her, and I decided to put thoughts of Travis to the back of my mind as much as I could and just enjoy having my daughter with me.

My plan to keep him at the back of my thoughts and take everything one day at a time seemed to work. The entire week went by without me seeing him once. Clearly, he had decided not to visit my bakery again, and I was more than fine with that.

But that Friday, everything went downhill rapidly.

Both Parker and Maggie were gone for the day, and I was cleaning up and getting ready to close the bakery. Amelia had taken up residence in one of the small booths in the seating area to the side of the space, and I heard her suddenly cry out.

I ran over to her and found her curled up on the bench, her arms wrapped tightly around her stomach as she sobbed. She'd had an upset stomach all day and had even rejected her favorite cookie and the sandwich I put on the menu just for her.

In the afternoon, I offered for her to go to my parents' house, but she said she just wanted to be near me. I knew that meant she felt really bad, but she insisted on staying there, so I just tried to get through the day as fast as I could.

Scooping her into my arms, I ran outside toward my car. As soon as I got her into the car seat and sat down behind the wheel, I called my mother to tell her what was going on.

CHAPTER 11

TRAVIS

The time had come for me to head out, and things had calmed considerably. I was dead tired and probably going to need a caffeine jolt just to power me back home. I headed into the breakroom and was disappointed to find that the coffee maker was completely empty. Figuring I should be the good guy who filled it back up, I did so and then turned to the fridge on the far wall. I would just have to do with a soda if I wanted some quick caffeine. Choosing a dark cola, I cracked it open and headed for the nurses' station to say goodnight.

Then I saw her.

Carrie was running in the doors of the emergency room down the hall. She was sobbing, and she was holding a little girl who was wailing. I sat the drink down and took off down the hall toward her before I realized what I was doing. All the discomfort, all the need to avoid her that I had was gone in that moment. All that mattered was her tears and the cry of the little girl curled up on her shoulder.

Questions zoomed through my mind at lightning speed,

but I shut them down. Was this her child? How old was she? Was she married now?

Snapping those questions down and stuffing them in a dark box in the corner of my mind, I went into doctor mode. I guided them into a triage room and placed my hand on Carrie's back to get her to the gurney. She laid the little girl down, and I yanked the stethoscope off the counter.

"How old is she?" I asked.

"Six," Carrie sobbed. "She's in so much pain."

"I can tell," I said and then turned my attention to the little girl. Her sobbing had slowed, and instead she had a steady stream of tears running down her cheeks but was remaining relatively quiet aside from occasional little whimpers. Something was itching in the back of my mind, but I ignored it. "What's your name, kiddo?"

"Amelia," she said. "It hurts."

"Where does it hurt, Amelia?"

"Here," Amelia said, pointing at the right lower side of her abdomen. "All the way to here." She continued motioning to her belly button.

"She's also been vomiting," Carrie said. "I don't know what's going on. Please, Travis, help her."

"It's going to be okay, Amelia. I'm Dr. King, and I'm going to make sure you get taken care of, okay?" The little girl nodded. "Okay, you just rest here for a few minutes, and I will be right back. I'm going to get you set up for some testing and we will figure out what's going on, don't you worry. Is it okay if I talk to your mommy for just a second? We will be right outside this door." She nodded again, and I motioned for Carrie to follow me.

"What is it?" Carrie asked as soon as the door was shut. "Is she going to be okay?"

"She's going to be fine, Carrie, don't worry," I said. I was still struggling with the emotions and thoughts going through my mind. "It looks like appendicitis."

"Oh, God," Carrie said.

"No, it's fine, seriously. It's a routine surgery, in and out. She will be okay. I just wanted you to be prepared if that's what it is, because it looks like it. I am going to go get her set up for surgery, and a nurse will be in with you in just a second, okay?"

"Okay," she said, and I turned to walk back to the nurse's desk when I felt a hand on my elbow. I turned to look into the tear-filled almond eyes that I had fallen in love with so many years ago. "Thank you, Travis."

I nodded and turned again, marching my way to the nurses' station with purpose so I didn't break down right then and there. Adrenaline was still pumping through me, and a nurse rushed in to see Amelia. I got on the phone and called Dr. Jones, who had just left. There was another doctor on call that night, but Dr. Jones was just minutes away, staying in the same apartments I had been placed in. He said he would be over momentarily, and I left to rejoin Carrie and Amelia in triage.

"We're going to move them to an actual room for surgery prep," I said as I came back in. The nurse nodded and flipped over a sheet on her clipboard. She was standing beside Carrie, who had her ID and her insurance card out.

"Thank you," the nurse said, turning back to Carrie. "Now, just a few more questions, okay? Father's name?"

There was a slight pause, and I felt my throat clutch shut.

"There isn't one," Carrie said, and I turned to look at her. We met eyes from across the little room, and then I looked down at a face that had some striking resemblances to my own.

72

She was six years old.

Six years.

Carrie was still staring at me defiantly. Six years and no dad.

I had to sit down. I slumped into a chair beside Amelia's bed. She had been looking at her mom, but now she turned to me. Her eyes were so hopeful, but I could see the pain behind them, and my heart clinched. Was it possible?

I had to shake it off. It didn't matter if it was possible. Or even probable. What mattered at that moment was helping a little girl who'd come in sick. The tests were administered and would only take a few minutes to get results back because the lab was in the hospital. While we waited, I avoided eye contact with Carrie, instead looking through the chart the nurse brought in with Amelia's medical history and pretending to find things to note. There was nothing to note. I just didn't want to stand in that withering glare from Carrie anymore. One that was filled with accusations and a dare. A dare to ask.

When the labs came back, I was grateful for the interruption and the break in tension in the room. The nurse swept in and handed them to me and then prepped the bed for the move to her own room out of triage. As we walked, I looked through the reports and made a few more notes. From the corner of my eye, I could see Carrie staring at me.

The notes were pretty clear. I didn't know if surgery was absolutely what Dr. Jones would say for right that moment, but I had about a 99 percent sure feeling it was. Scooting the chair closer to Amelia, I looked over her tiny little body to her mother. Carrie was attentive, and her eyes had softened some, but not much. There were still many words unsaid between us, but they would have to wait. For now.

"So," I said, addressing Amelia. "It looks like this tiny little organ in your tummy is causing all this pain you're having." I pointed to the area where the appendix was located.

Amelia nodded. "That's where it hurts."

I smiled down at her. "I know, kiddo. We're going to get that little pest out of your tummy and fix you right up."

Amelia's eyes went wide, and her mother stood to hold her hand.

"It's okay, baby," Carrie said.

"It is, it's okay. It's a no-big-deal surgery," I said. It wasn't a complete lie. "And afterward, you will get to hang out here for a little bit, and you might even be able to go home tonight. If not, I will see you in the morning bright and early."

"What happens with an appendectomy, exactly?" Carrie asked.

"Well, the surgeon will make a tiny incision here," I began but was interrupted when the door slammed open. I turned to see the surprised, then incensed faces of Mr. and Mrs. Jacobs.

"You," Mr. Jacobs said.

"Hello, Mr. Jacobs. Dr. Jones should be here in a matter of moments. In fact, there he is," I said, motioning behind Mrs. Jones, who still stood in the doorway.

"Ah, hello, Dr. King," he said. "Surprised you are still here. I hear you've done a marvelous job caring for our little guest?"

"She is a trooper, Doc. Tough as nails," I said, getting a tiny smile from Amelia's face. She had a dimple I recognized from every time I looked in a mirror. I risked another glance at Carrie, who looked on the edge of tears again.

"Right, then," Dr. Jones said. "You have the labs?" I

handed them over, and he took a look at them. "I trust your judgment here, Dr. King. Open appendectomy seems appropriate."

"What about antibiotics?" I asked.

"Do you think that would be suitable?" Dr. Jones asked. There was something in his voice that made me think he knew something was up. It was as if he were intentionally treating me as an equal, and verbally in front of Carrie and her parents. It might have just been an attempt to look like we were exhausting every other effort before surgery, but there was another element to it I couldn't put my finger on. Either way, it seemed to calm her parents somewhat.

"Frankly, no," I said. "She is extraordinarily brave and strong, so I think we should just go ahead and do the surgery and get the appendix out. She's not scared."

"Oh my, she is a brave one," Dr. Jones said, getting another smile from Carrie. "If I could have a moment with Miss Jacobs and Amelia," he said, indicating her parents.

"Sorry, these are my parents," Carrie said.

"Lovely to meet you," Dr. Jones said. "There is a waiting room just down the hall if you would like. We will be heading in for surgery in just a few minutes."

They seemed to take the hint and walked out of the room, glaring at me as they went. When they were gone, Dr. Jones turned to me too. His voice grew quiet and more serious.

"Are you alright, son?" he asked.

"Yeah, fine," I said. He nodded and clicked the roof of his mouth with his tongue.

"Good. Well," he said, "I think you should go on home and get some sleep. You were supposed to be off."

"So were you."

He laughed. "I am never off, my boy. Go on, get out of here."

I nodded and then went up to Amelia one last time. She had already started receiving antibiotics and a mild pain reliever. She was trying to be brave but kept looking at the IV in her arm.

"Okay, little one. I'm heading out, but I am leaving you in the hands of Dr. Jones. He is the person I trust most in this hospital, and he will take great care of you," I said. "I will see you in the morning if you're still here. If not, then I hope to see you again soon and see how you're doing." I said that last sentence to Carrie, who made no indication either way.

With that, I headed out and watched as they wheeled her through the double doors leading to the surgical suite. I had so many questions, but I wasn't going to get any answers just then.

I was supposed to be off, Dr. Jones said, so I was. I clocked out again and headed back to the apartment to think about it all. Hopefully I would be able to get some sleep tonight, but I doubted it. One thing I knew was I would be making another call to my sponsor.

CHAPTER 12

CARRIE

My mind was spinning so fast my thoughts were little more than a blur of colors across the backs of my eyes. I couldn't focus. I couldn't get any thought to stay still long enough for me to know what it was. I didn't know what to feel or what I was supposed to do next.

I'd never been through something like this before. Amelia had always been an extremely healthy child. My pregnancy was smooth and easy. She was born pink and screaming just the way she was supposed to. I could count the number of times she'd had a cold or ear infection in her entire life on one hand. She wasn't accident-prone, never had a cavity. The last time she was in a hospital was her checkup three days after she was born.

It meant I was completely unprepared to handle something like this. I knew she was in good hands and the doctor would take good care of her. But all I could think was that my baby was somewhere in the back of the hospital and I wasn't with her. She needed me, and I couldn't be there beside her.

It made my heart ache, and the anxiety built up in me so

much I couldn't sit still. Every time a door opened, or I saw a new person out of the corner of my eye, my attention snapped to them, waiting to hear something about Amelia. I had finally spotted my mother after pacing around for a few minutes.

I rushed over to her, and she gathered me up in a hug. "What's going on?"

Tears stung my eyes, but I was trying to hold them back. I knew if I let them out, I wouldn't be able to get them back under control. Right now, I needed to be as put together as possible, ready to make any decision I needed to. I had to be able to understand what was going on and react quickly if the doctor came out to talk to me about Amelia.

"It's appendicitis," I said. "We were at the bakery, and she said her stomach was hurting, but she didn't want to go home or to your house. She just wanted to be near me. So, I had her in one of the booths in the front. She seemed to be doing okay and was stretched out on the bench when she just suddenly started crying. She was clutching her stomach, and I didn't know what to do."

I was starting to hyperventilate, and Mom reached out to grab me by my upper arms and steady me. She forced me to look into her face.

"Calm down," she said. "Just take a deep breath and tell me what happened."

I forced my lungs to accept a breath and let it out as slowly as I could. When I started talking again, my voice sounded steadier.

"She looked like she was in so much pain and then she started vomiting. It was awful. I got her in the car and came here. It was the only thing I could think to do. This wasn't a normal stomachache," I said.

"No, you did the right thing," Mom said. "What have they said? Where is she now?"

"They just said it was appendicitis and they needed to operate. She's in surgery now."

Mom nodded. "She's in good hands. She's going to be alright. At least you caught it before it got any more serious." She smoothed my hair away from my face and looked around. "So you've spoken to Travis?"

I stared at her, not believing that was really what was on her mind at that moment. Stepping back from her, I started pacing again. This wasn't the time to be thinking about Travis or what he might be thinking. I saw him, and of course, he saw Amelia. But right then, I didn't care. Worrying about what he might be thinking or if he had figured out her parentage was the furthest thing from my mind.

All I was thinking about was my little girl going through the biggest challenge of her life and feeling nothing short of helpless.

"Carrie," my mother said, taking a step toward me. "If he saw you..."

I held up a hand. "Not right now, Mom."

Walking over to the station across the waiting room, I made myself a cup of coffee. My hand shook as I sipped it, but the hot liquid felt soothing going down my throat. I wrapped my hands around the mug and carried it with me as I continued to a pace across the waiting room.

A few more times as we waited, my mother tried to start the conversation about Travis. Each time, I shushed her, not willing to venture into that until we knew what was going on. There wasn't enough space in my brain to deal with both situations, and like always, Amelia would come first. She always had, and she always would.

It felt like I paced through that waiting room for the entire day, but I later realized it was only an hour after my mother arrived when the doctor finally came out. As soon as I saw him, I rushed toward him, desperate to hear anything. I was terrified, my heart racing so hard in my chest I thought it might burst out at any moment. But when I got closer to the doctor, I could see the expression on his face looked like he had good news.

"She's doing great," Dr. Jones said.

Relief rushed over me, and I felt tension flow out of my shoulders and neck as a hesitant smile crossed my face.

"The surgery went well?" I asked.

He nodded. "It went perfectly. I'm definitely glad you got her in as quickly as you did. Things could have gotten much worse if much more time passed. But the good thing is, that didn't happen. She got here, and we were able to get in there and fix the issue perfectly. She was an absolute trooper and is in recovery now."

"Can I go see her?"

"Absolutely. She's getting moved into her recovery room right now. Just give us a couple minutes and I will bring you back there. Hang tight."

"Thank you so much, Doctor," I said.

"You're very welcome."

He shook my hand with a warm smile before heading back through the door out of the waiting room. I turned to my mother, and she wrapped me in another tight hug. I had never felt relief like that before. After so much fear and worry, the worst was over, and I could start to feel better again.

"She's going to be okay," Mom said.

I didn't want her to ask about Travis again. I stepped away from her to send a text to Maggie and Parker to let them know everything was alright. I had messaged them after Amelia went into surgery, wanting to make sure they knew what was going on in case I wasn't able to get to the bakery for the next few days.

It was enough of a distraction to keep Mom from mentioning Travis before the doctor came back into the waiting room. I immediately crossed the room to follow him to the recovery area where they had Amelia.

"I'll go ahead and warn you that she is not awake yet. That's on purpose. We are keeping her sedated for a little while longer just to give her body time to rest and recover. Her vitals look fantastic, and we're keeping a close watch on her, so you don't have to worry. I just didn't want you to expect to go in there and find her awake and ready to talk," the doctor said.

I nodded. He opened the door, and we walked inside. My little girl looked smaller and so vulnerable in the hospital bed. The blankets swallowed her up, and I hated to see the IV in her arm. I went to the side of the bed and ran my hand along her face. Leaning down, I kissed both of her cheeks.

"Mama's here," I whispered to her. "I love you."

"She's going to have to stay here for recovery and observation for a little while. I can't give you an exact timeline. It's all about how she does, but with how she's getting through right now, I don't think it's going to be a long stay. She'll need a lot of rest while she's recovering. Unfortunately, there will be some pain and discomfort for a little while. But it shouldn't be too bad. We'll go over everything when I come back to check in on her tomorrow. For now, just know that she's doing just fine," Dr. Jones said.

"Thank you," I said.

He nodded and walked out of the room, closing the

door behind him. I sat down in the chair beside Amelia's bed and held her hand. Within seconds of it being just my mother and me in the room with my sleeping daughter, I couldn't hold back my emotions anymore. I let out the sobs I'd been holding back since getting to the hospital.

It was the most terrifying experience of my life. Far worse than anything else I had ever experienced. My mother crouched down beside me and wrapped her arms around me, holding me as I got out all my emotion. Rather than trying to control it, I just let it all out.

Finally, I got myself together enough to wipe off my face and take a few calming breaths. I looked around me.

"I don't know what happened to my coffee," I said.

I knew I had some when I was in the waiting room, but I couldn't figure out what I did with it in between making it for myself and coming back here with the doctor. Mom patted me on the hand.

"Don't worry. I'll get you some more. I'll be right back."

While she was gone, I stared down at my daughter. She was so sweet, so innocent. I hated knowing she had to go through all of this without me being able to help her. She would feel sick and be in pain, and there would be nothing I could do to make it go away. I hated that feeling. I wanted to be able to take it all on, to make sure she never had to go through any of it. But I knew I couldn't. All I could do was make sure I was there for her and do anything possible to make her more comfortable.

It was a moment of clarity as I watched her sleep.

When Mom came back into the room, she handed me a cup of coffee, and I took a grateful sip. She settled onto the small couch to the side of the room and watched me for a few seconds. Finally, she looked down into her own cup, then back up at me.

"We have to talk about this now. I understand that you didn't want to talk about it while you were waiting to find out about her surgery, but she has gotten through it and is recovering well now. It's time to deal with this situation."

"I agree," I said.

"So, you did see Travis, I'm assuming. If he's doing his residency here in pediatrics, it would make sense you would see him when you came in."

"Yes. I saw him."

"Did he say anything?"

I shook my head. "No. But that doesn't mean anything. With all the chaos going on, it really wasn't the time for him to say anything. But I do think he has probably put it together. He looked right at her. It isn't hard to see the similarities. I don't think I have a choice anymore. I'm going to have to talk to him about this."

Her expression became concerned, and she shook her head. "Don't make any rash decisions, Carrie. Until you absolutely confirm it, he doesn't know anything. You can still keep this a secret. We can maintain everything the way it has been."

"No, Mom. I don't think we can. We've been hanging on to this secret for seven years, and it hasn't been all that hard because he hasn't been around. That's not the case anymore. He's here, and he's not going anywhere anytime soon. I can't keep this a secret anymore. And to tell you the truth, I'm not sure I want to."

CHAPTER 13

TRAVIS

I didn't want to get out of bed. It was Saturday morning, and again I had it off. Why Dr. Jones had chosen to give me Saturdays off was still a mystery to me, but it was nice to have a day off that most of the rest of the world had off too. I still needed to adjust to the schedule of my new life, though, and after everything that happened last night, it was probably a good idea to stay in bed as long as I needed and get the rest. But as much as I didn't want to leave the comfortable cocoon I'd created for myself, I knew I couldn't stay there.

I had been on the phone with my sponsor until the early morning. Far past the window I normally crashed, she and I talked. She was a wonderful sounding board, an older lady in her sixties who had started drinking in her teens like me. She knew the ins and outs of the desire to drink better than anyone, and also knew what it was like to navigate through her sobriety even in the tough times.

I shook my head and went over the conversation in my mind, letting her words sink into me.

"Travis, you know I know you better than you seem to know yourself," she said.

"I know," I had responded.

"And I know how you tend to shut the world off when you are uncomfortable, and that leads to finding other ways to pass the time. And what are idle hands, Travis?"

"The devil's playthings."

"Exactly," she said. "In our case, that means devil water. That's our curse. But the best way to fight that is to keep those hands busy. Keep that mind busy. You need to get out there and meet some people."

"I can't," I said. "This town is full of people who knew my folks."

"Oh, who cares?" she said. "They don't know you. Not yet. If you meet them and make the right impression, they will never worry about who your parents were or weren't. You need to trust people to come into your life."

"I don't know," I had said. "I just want to get this residency done and leave this place behind for good."

As the words came out of my mouth, I realized how bitter they tasted. The more I tried to think about Monroe, the more resolved I grew to get far away from it. And yet, it seemed harder and harder to think about what a life would be outside of this town. What would I do? How would I go on with my life knowing what I knew? Or at least suspecting what I suspected?

Rolling out of bed that morning, I was groggy and sore. The fast-paced life on my feet was starting to get to the stage where my body just had to adjust and deal with it, and the transition was a pain. It would take a few more days before being on my feet that long would be normal, and I wouldn't feel it. At that moment, I felt it.

Even though it wasn't on my schedule, I had made a promise to little Amelia that I would stop by in the morning. My suspicions were at an all-time high, and I found myself worried about her, even though I barely knew her and was completely sure her surgery would have gone flawlessly. But even more than that, there was someone else I wanted to see.

Glancing at the clock, I saw it was still early, and I grabbed my work scrubs just in case. Getting a nice warm shower to wake me up and get me going, I put on some jeans and a T-shirt with a hoodie and took the bag with the scrubs with me. Deciding just to walk across the campus, I kept my head down and my mind in the clouds. Before long I was standing just outside the main building doors, and I still didn't know what I was going to say or how to say them. I took a deep breath and walked inside.

Several people I knew were milling around and greeted me somewhat confusedly. Either they knew I was off that day or were puzzled by my street clothes, but thankfully, no one questioned me on my presence. I made my way through the hospital to the nurses' desk and asked for the room number for Amelia.

"Morning," I said as I reached the nurses' desk. "What room is Amelia Jacobs in?"

"Morning," a voice responded from below the desk. "Aren't you off today?" Rhea, one of the nurses, asked. She placed some papers on the desk that she had been bending over to get.

"Supposed to be," I said, hoping she wouldn't investigate any further.

"Overachiever, eh? Well, they're back in room six," she said. Her expression was one of critical curiosity, but she didn't actually say anything, so I headed off to see Amelia.

I wasn't prepared for the glimpse into the room that I

got. Carrie was sitting in a chair by the window, just at the foot of the bed. She was slumped over, clearly asleep. A handmade blanket that I recognized as one her grandmother made her when we were dating was draped over her shoulder, and she was leaning her head on a tiny pillow like the ones the hospital kept on the couches out in the waiting room.

I reached for the chart on the wall by the door and pulled it down. Technically, I wasn't supposed to read it without being on duty, but I didn't think anyone was going to mind. I opened it up and saw that Amelia had had her surgery and that everything had gone perfectly. If her labs continued to show that she was doing well, she should be able to go home sometime today.

Sliding the chart back onto the wall, a flood of emotion started to hit me. As much as I had tried to avoid Carrie, there she was. Just feet away from me. Of course, the kid complicated everything, and that was even if I was getting the math wrong. But I didn't think I was. Everything seemed to point to the obvious, and I had to prepare myself for learning that truth.

Sudden terror gripped me. When I opened that door, there was no way out of knowing the truth. I was going to know if that little girl was mine or not, and it wasn't something I could un-know. I couldn't just go about my life and pretend I hadn't seen her, hadn't talked to her, didn't know she was mine. Not if she was. I was going to have to live with the knowledge that, if she was mine, Carrie had her after I left her without an explanation. If it was true, I was the worst kind of person.

But I needed to know. I couldn't turn around and walk out of the hospital, even though part of me wanted to and was screaming to do it. It was my day off. I could roll out the door and go back to bed and pretend this was all just a terrible dream. But I knew that if I did that, I wouldn't be able to stay here. I would have to transfer or quit the program. My dreams would be gone. The only option forward was to find out and deal with the consequences.

Sighing, I took one more look through the window. It didn't surprise me that Dr. Jones let Carrie spend the night. He seemed to intuitively know something was up, and I had a sneaking suspicion that he knew what was coming.

I took another couple of breaths to try to calm the pounding of my heart. I wrapped my fingers around the knob and turned, leaving the old me on one side of the door and a new me, a me that would know for sure if he was a father, on the other.

Was I ready for this?

CHAPTER 14

CARRIE

My mother stayed with me for a few hours. She wasn't happy about the decision I was making about Travis, and I knew she probably hoped I would change my mind about it once I was in a less emotional state.

She hadn't been Travis' biggest fan when we were together, and the feeling only increased when I found out I was pregnant. There was never even the slightest hint of animosity toward Amelia or the sense that she didn't want her. My daughter was the light of my parents' lives. They just preferred to pretend I'd managed to produce her completely on my own.

The thought of bringing Travis into our lives wasn't something she wanted to think about. Both my parents were supportive of me not telling Travis about the pregnancy from the very beginning, and that support never faltered. There was never a second when they wondered if I was doing the wrong thing or suggested I tell Amelia about her father. It was always just understood that we were the family she would know.

Now that was changing. She was going to have to accept that Travis deserved to know about his daughter. Even beyond that, he probably already knew about her. Just looking at her was enough to create some suspicions. But he also knew how old she was. Unless he was going to make the assumption that I cheated on him, he would be able to piece it together.

Even with the argument between us, my mother stayed to support me and be there for Amelia. As the afternoon turned to evening, she started getting ready to go home to my father.

"You should go on home," she said. "Get some rest."

"I need to be here with her," I said. "We've never been apart overnight."

"I know," Mom said. "You end up on the couch every time Amelia tries to have a sleepover at my house. But you know she's safe here. They're going to take good care of her. You should go home and sleep. You know you'll feel better in the morning if you're able to get up and get a shower."

This was true. At least, I would feel physically better. But there was no way I could be away from my daughter. Not while she was lying in a hospital. It didn't matter how I felt. No discomfort was enough to make me want to leave her. And I couldn't bear the thought of her waking up and me not being there.

"No. I'm going to stay here. The nursing staff already said it would be okay. They're going to bring me a pillow and some blankets. It's going to be fine. I don't know when she might wake up, and I don't want her to be alone when she does," I said.

"You're a good mother."

Mom leaned down and kissed me on top of the head. It was much more of a show of affection than I was used to from her now that I was an adult, but the situation seemed to warrant it. Her comment on my mothering hung heavy in the air. It didn't just feel like she was talking about me staying at the hospital with Amelia. There was something else behind that statement. She just wasn't going to elaborate on it.

After my mother left, I called my best friend, Tina, to give her another update. It wasn't long before she showed up with dinner for us. She stayed to eat with me, and we talked about all the inane little things best friends can talk about and somehow make it interesting. Playful gossip and updates on what was and wasn't going on in life eased my tension and helped me to feel more relaxed.

Tina gave me the same recommendation as my mother to go home but was quicker to relent when I said I wasn't leaving. I promised to call her the next day to let her know what was going on, then followed her out so I could go to the nurses' station and ask for the bedding.

The small sofa definitely wasn't designed for long-term comfort, but I didn't care. I was close to Amelia.

My alarm woke me up as usual, and I scrambled to silence it as quickly as possible so it didn't disturb Amelia. The nurses told me the medication was going to wear off and she would be waking up on her own sometime in the morning. I wanted to give her the chance to ease out of sleep when it was right for her rather than being startled out of it.

I glanced over at her, and she shifted but didn't wake up. Going into the small bathroom attached to the room, I freshened up as best I could. When I got out, I called my mother to let her know Amelia hadn't woken up yet.

"What are you going to do about the bakery?" Mom asked.

"Maggie and Parker already know what's going on. They're going to have to hold down the fort until I can leave the hospital," I said.

"I'll go up there and help out."

"Really?" I asked.

"Of course. Remember, a lot of those recipes people know you for came right from my grandmother and her mother before her. And a couple of them even came from me," she said.

"I know. I just don't want to put you out," I said.

"You're not. It will be fun."

I didn't necessarily believe she would find the whole experience fun, exactly, but I didn't argue. Behind me, I heard a knock on the door.

"I've got to go, Mom. Dr. Jones is here to check on Amelia. Thank you so much for helping out at the bakery. I'll let you know what's going on," I said.

We said our goodbyes, and I tucked my phone away in my pocket. The doctor already told me he would come back to check on Amelia in the morning, so I wasn't surprised to hear the knock. The surprise came after I called out for Dr. Jones to come in, and the door opened to show Travis in the doorway.

My mouth fell open slightly, but nothing came out. He hesitated there for only a second, then stepped in and closed the door behind him.

"How is she?" Travis asked.

"Doing well. Dr. Jones said she got through the surgery perfectly, and it looks like her recovery will go smoothly."

"That's good to hear."

He looked around me to the bed, and I knew this was the time. I couldn't wait anymore. I had to tell him the truth.

"Travis, we need to talk," I said.

I wished I could have come up with some sort of smoother introduction, but those were the words that formed when I opened my mouth.

"Carrie, I know," he said.

My heart felt like it stopped for a few seconds as I stared at him. I spent a moment trying to smooth my hair out, but I knew I was just wasting time. Glancing behind me at the bed, I let out a breath and turned back to Travis.

"You know?" I asked.

He gave a slight shrug and nodded. "I did the math. She's about six?"

I nodded. Just as I expected, Travis hadn't missed anything when he saw Amelia. I was relieved to know his mind hadn't jumped immediately to the possibility that I'd cheated on him. If he had said something like that, I didn't know how I would handle it.

"I found out I was pregnant the day after you left. I realized I had missed my period, and I wasn't feeling well, so my mother brought me to the doctor. It came as a complete shock," I said.

"That I can definitely understand," he said.

I had a feeling he was talking about himself as much as he was talking about me. It had to be an incredible shock for him. At least mine came with the knowledge I had several months to prepare before my child arrived. Travis didn't get that. One moment he had no idea he was a father, then in the next he was facing the reality that he had a child.

"I decided right then not to tell you. You'd already left, and even though I probably could have told your parents and had them pass it along, I figured it didn't really matter. You had made your decision and you weren't answering any of my calls. I didn't want to make it any more confusing or more challenging than it already was," I said.

"How long were you going to keep it from me? I mean, did you ever plan on telling me?" Travis asked.

"Honestly, I had no plan to tell you. I probably never would have if you hadn't come back."

I saw him wince at that statement, but I couldn't back down. I needed to tell him everything. This wasn't just about me coming clean and letting him know he had a daughter. We needed to get everything out in the open so we could figure out what was going to happen moving forward.

My main worry was that Travis would want custody, and he would fight for Amelia.

"You were just suddenly gone, and I had no idea where you were or how to get in touch with you. I went to see your parents before I found out, and they weren't able to tell me anything. It occurred to me that I couldn't really see any good coming out of telling you. Even if I had been able to find you," I said.

"What do you mean?"

"If I had been able to track you down early on and told you, I honestly didn't think there would be any benefit to it. You obviously didn't want anything to do with me, so why would you want anything to do with our child? You needed to go and find whatever it was you were after, and that didn't include suddenly becoming a father."

"And then the years after? When you could have found me?" he asked.

"I didn't think you would ever come back. I thought it would be better and easier for everyone involved if I just kept everything separated. You were gone and we weren't together. That seemed like too much complication and unnecessary drama to deal with. I don't expect you to understand how I was feeling. It wasn't an easy time." I drew in a breath. "Right now, my biggest worry is that this is about to become messy. I'm worried you're going to want custody and will fight me for her."

"When I decided to come back here to do my residency, the plan was never to stay. I intended to get through the three years and go settle somewhere else. But now, this is something I need time to think about," he said.

"I understand," I said.

"Carrie, I promise I will respect your wishes when it comes to her. I don't feel the need to try to tear her away from you."

Taking in what he said left me in an unbalanced moment. Knowing Travis wasn't going to fight for her was a relief. And this settled something in me, but it also fed into my long-held anger and hurt with regards to him. He never did fight for her. For either of us.

CHAPTER 15

TRAVIS

I was in a daze as I walked away from the room. Making my way through the hospital, I found myself in the cafeteria before I realized I had just been wandering around, lost in my thoughts. My stomach rumbled, and I decided to grab a sandwich to take with me wherever it was I went. Standing in line felt surreal. My heart was racing, and I had the panicky feeling that I needed to drop everything and run. But where? Where would I run to? I didn't know and couldn't come up with an answer, so I just stayed in line.

After I paid for my sandwich and drink, I took them with me on the walk back to the apartment. It was only about a half a mile, but it felt like it might as well have been across the entire country. I simultaneously felt like I had all the energy in the world and that I just wanted to crash in bed and sleep for days. I had a kid. With Carrie. What the hell was I going to do?

As I rounded the corner of my street and saw the apartment in the distance, I made a choice, albeit one I didn't seem to put much thought into. I had my keys. I was going to drive somewhere. I wasn't sure where, but I was going to get in the car and turn on the ignition and put it in drive. Any more planning than that was just simply too much for me to do.

Suddenly, I found myself driving. It was as if time had just passed, and I found myself in the car, on the road, pulling down a street I knew so well. I hadn't meant to come here. I had just started driving, and my brain went to default, pulling me along roads and side roads until it brought me to a place it knew. A place it could get to without instruction.

My parents' house.

I pulled into the driveway and put the car into park. I didn't bother to turn the car off because I didn't figure I would get out of it. I wasn't there to go inside and wander around. I just needed a place to think.

My eyes trailed over the building, and I noticed it didn't look too bad. I didn't know exactly what I was expecting, really. It was a suburban street, so vandalism wasn't likely to be a big problem. I'd had the house emptied of valuables years before, leaving only scant furniture I didn't feel like paying to have disposed of or stored. Mostly, though, the house was empty. Anything important had been kept or given away to Hank or some of Mom and Dad's other friends. Anything else had been tossed or given to charity. A few boxes of things were in a storage unit that I paid for in town. I hadn't done any of the moving, so I wasn't sure what exactly was in it.

I was out of the car now, though the key was still in the ignition. The rest of the keychain was in my hand, and I looked down at it. At some point I had wiggled the car key off it and didn't remember doing it. The fog of my brain was thick, and I was operating almost solely on autopilot. I found the key that I inexplicably kept on my regular keychain and slid it into the front door. It opened easily, and I walked inside.

The house was cold and empty. One small, beaten-up couch sat against a wall in the living room. A few folded-up empty boxes sat beside it, as if they were there for the packing and turned out not to be needed. They had a thick layer of dust on them that told me they had been here for years. I looked to the right and saw the kitchen and beyond it the stairs. Cabinet doors were open in the kitchen, but they were completely empty. The stairs led to rooms that were also open and empty. Bug bombs sat in various areas of the house, long since used.

It dawned on me that Hank had been in charge of keeping the house up a little. I had asked him over a phone call years back to do it. He had the spare key that was always kept in the backyard under the heavy ceramic frog. He was only supposed to come in once in a while, make sure the electricity stayed on and the water was still running and that things weren't falling completely apart. In case I wanted to sell it. Bug bombs were part of that too.

I shivered in the cold. The thermostat read that it was rather chilly and hadn't been set to come on unless it got to an emergency level far below comfortable living. It was only on at all to keep the pipes from freezing. Instinctively, I cut it on, turning the heat up to the low sixties. Then I hung my head.

I couldn't stay there. I knew that. The longer I stayed inside that house, the more I spiraled. It wouldn't be long before I would be standing in the living room, a fifth of vodka in one hand and a glass of orange juice in the other. Eventually the orange juice would run out before the vodka, and I would give up all pretense. Then I would end up doing something truly stupid.

My own weakness disgusted me. I had been sober for years, and just stepping foot in Monroe was like walking into a bar where all the waitresses knew my name and all my favorite drinks were free. It tempted me to the bottle like a moth to flame, and I didn't know why I couldn't just ignore the siren call. Why couldn't I walk into my parents' house, the house I had spent so much time in, and not feel the need to stop at the bar on the way wherever I went after? Why couldn't I just be normal?

Being in Monroe, being in this house, it made me want to be who they thought I was anyway. It made a spiteful part of me want to just lean in and be who they assumed I would always grow up to be, no matter how much I had fought it before. Fuck it. It would make them happy.

My head was screwed up. I needed to go.

I walked outside and stared across the street. Two streets behind the house that was directly across from me was Carrie's parents' house. It wasn't far, but enough that in the cold you wanted to drive the distance. Or at least I had when I was young and happy to have any excuse to drive. I had also spent many happy days walking between the two houses too. It was a path I knew so well, I was sure I could walk it, even now, in my dreamlike daze.

Everything stung. Everything hurt. Everything was targeted right at my soul. I had to get out of there, fast.

I shut the door and locked it, headed down to the car, and hopped inside. It was nice and toasty in the car, and I took off my gloves and pulled out of the driveway. I wasn't sure where I was going until I was almost there, and when I pulled in, I hoped I could make it work. I had been really curt and rude the last time I had spoken to Hank, and yet here I was, coming back to his house and hoping for some guidance. Or at least someone to talk to.

Hank had been Dad's friend, that was true, but he was also a good man. A man I felt like I could trust to give me frank advice that maybe I wouldn't like to hear but needed to.

I pulled up to his house and parked the car. I tried to think of how to address what was going on and couldn't put it into words. I had a kid. This was part of it. But also, part of it was Carrie never telling me. No one ever telling me. I had been going for years building my life and making something of myself, and now I was getting hit with the bombshell that I had a little girl. Not a baby, but a full-on child. I had missed so much of her life, so many milestones. I would have missed all of them, had Carrie had her way. She'd never planned on telling me, I knew. Me coming back here to work at the hospital had ruined her plan.

Maybe it was better with me gone. Maybe me being away on the other side of the country had given us both the life we needed to have. For me it was solitude and distance from my shit childhood, from my parents. It was sobriety that was easy to maintain and a life that was full, if lonely. A life that was busy, if a little sad.

For her it meant living in her hometown with our baby. A baby that undoubtedly would remind her of me often and the relationship I had skipped out on. Her own daughter would remind her of that pain that I was sure I'd caused her. I was a monster for that. But she had a life in Monroe, friends and family that could help her. She had a business. She seemed like she might be happy. All I had done was cause her trouble and then leave her pregnant.

But could I leave now that I knew? I had a plan, one that I was dead set on pursuing. I was going to finish my residency and get the hell out of town for good. Never, ever look back. If I had to give my parents' house away, just to be rid of it, I would. I could just up and leave and be somewhere that I could find a life after residency and work to make some other corner of the globe better because of me rather than stay in Monroe and make myself worse because of the town.

Yet, as much as I knew that was my plan, as absolutely certain of it that I was just weeks ago, all of that had changed now. I had a little girl, one that reminded me of myself, my parents, the future I left behind. I couldn't just leave all that, could I?

I stepped out of the car and walked up the long driveway to Hank's house. It was a half-circle, and his porch had steps on either side, so I chose the one closest to me and walked up them. Usually, with Hank, you didn't have to knock because he would have seen you coming, but since it was early on a Saturday, there was a chance he was sleeping in. I made it all the way to the door and knocked.

A shuffling sound behind the door could be heard just before the locks began to fall. Hank was many things, and mild conspiracy theorist was one of them. Having several chain locks and key locks on his door was something he prided himself on, though I didn't have the heart to tell him his windows were giant signs saying "break me" to anyone that really wanted inside. Not that I would know who would.

"Travis?" he asked as he opened the door in his bathrobe and saw me. "What are you doing here?"

"I came to apologize," I said. "Can I come in?"

CHAPTER 16

CARRIE

The night Amelia had to stay in the hospital recovering felt like the longest day of my life. I knew she was doing well and the doctors were taking exceptional care of her, but I just wanted to get her home. Them discharging her would mean she was doing better, that she was strong and well on her way to recovery. It was what I needed.

In the morning when I woke up on that tight couch, I called my mother to make sure she was going to the bakery. Later in the afternoon, Amelia and I would call together and video chat with her, Maggie, and Parker. Even if she were still looking a little tired and like she didn't feel great, my little girl still lit up when she got to see them, so I knew it would lift her spirits. I also knew she was looking forward to getting out and being back in the bakery where she loved to be.

But the most difficult moment came when Travis showed back up at the door to her room. He looked at me questioningly, and I already knew what he was thinking. This was something that we'd always had in our relationship. We could communicate with each other just through a look.

And that look said he wanted to know more. I wasn't ready for a full introduction yet. This wasn't the time, and it definitely wasn't the place. Amelia was literally confined to a bed. She didn't have any chance to really interact, and if she was uncomfortable, there was nothing we could do about it. It wasn't like I would be able to pack her up and get her away from the situation.

I also couldn't just tell him to leave. It would be a bad start to what I knew would eventually have to be the two of them getting to know each other. I knew I couldn't keep them apart anymore. I didn't know what was in the future. I just knew it had to move forward.

But I was going to be the one in control. In the end, I was still Amelia's mother. And it was my responsibility to protect her, which meant taking this one careful step at a time. After leaving for a few hours, he had returned and stuck his head through the door. While he was out, Amelia had woken up, and I figured there was no pushing it off anymore.

"Can I come in?" Travis asked.

I nodded and he stepped the rest of the way in. Amelia was sitting up coloring in a book my mother had brought by for her the evening before and barely glanced up. He stepped up toward me, and I walked over to the side of the bed. Smoothing her hair back, I leaned down slightly toward Amelia.

"Baby, there's someone here to see you," I said. She put her coloring down and looked up at me. I gestured toward Travis. "This is Dr. King. Do you remember him from before the surgery? He's a very old friend of mine."

She smiled at him. "Hi." She then turned to me and shook her head. "I don't remember, Mommy."

His lips twitched, and a blend of emotions came over his eyes. He took another step toward the bed.

"Hi, Amelia. How are you feeling?" he asked cautiously.

"Better. My tummy doesn't hurt anymore. But where they cut me open does a little," she said.

He nodded. "That must have been scary. But I heard from Dr. Jones that you were very brave."

"You're a doctor too?" she asked.

"I am," he said. "I was the person who first saw you when you came in."

"I don't really remember that," she admitted.

"It's okay. You were in a lot of pain when your mama brought you here. I'm just glad you're doing better."

She smiled at Travis, and I swear I could see his heart swell in his chest. I knew the feeling well.

Travis looked over at me, and I gave a slight nod. He looked back at Amelia. "I have to go now. But maybe I'll see you again."

"Okay," she said happily. "I'm leaving soon. But maybe you can visit."

He let out a hint of a laugh. "I'd like that."

"I'll be right back," I said to Amelia, and she nodded as she went back to her coloring.

We walked out of the room, and I closed the door most of the way behind me so she couldn't hear us talking.

"I'm surprised she doesn't remember you when we came in," I said.

"I'm not," Travis said. "She was in a lot of pain, and then they put her on some heavy-duty drugs. I'm not offended."

"Oh, I guess that makes sense."

"What happens next?"

"Let me get her home and back into her routine. Then we'll figure something out. I'll get in touch with you," I said.

We exchanged phone numbers, and then he paused for just a second like he was thinking about something else to say before turning and walking away.

The next morning, Amelia was finally discharged, and I was able to bring her home to keep recovering.

Over the next couple of days, I realized that with my daughter home and getting better, I had a lot more time on my hands. I didn't want to go back to the bakery until she was feeling up to going with me, and she was still sleeping a lot. This meant I was left with a lot of time and quiet to figure out what I was going to do next.

A big part of me just wanted to ignore Travis. I wanted to go back to taking my parents' advice and continuing on just the way we had been, only with the knowledge that Travis knew now. But that wasn't realistic. Amelia had been asking questions I didn't know how to answer, and her plea to Santa this past Christmas left my heart aching. She had told me she asked him to bring her a daddy.

Besides, it wasn't like it was at the beginning when I first made the decision. Travis was here now. Didn't he have the right to know his daughter?

It was the very question that was bouncing around in my head. I knew my parents didn't think so, but that wasn't that much of a surprise. They never agreed with my relationship with Travis. They never thought he was good enough for me, even when I was happy and things were great between us.

Then he proved them right by leaving me.

But now. Now, he was here. He was in town, part of my existence again. And that changed everything.

Finally, I called Tina. Right then, I needed support, not judgment. I loved my mother, but she couldn't give me what I really needed in this situation. I needed my best friend. Fortunately, Tina had just gotten back in town after going to visit family in Chicago for a few days. She hadn't wanted to leave Amelia and me, but she had the trip planned for a long time, and I insisted she go.

Now I was glad it was just a short visit and I could have her come over. I had been holding everything in since she left, not wanting to talk about it over the phone. As soon as I called to tell her I had a lot to talk to her about, she said she was on her way, and I felt myself relax a little.

Amelia had taken her medication and was in bed by the time Tina arrived. I opened the door and found her with ice cream and a big smile.

"How's Amelia?" she asked as we made our way to the kitchen. "I brought her favorite flavor and toppings."

"She's asleep. The medication makes her really tired, and the doctor said she needs to get as much sleep as possible while she's recovering. But I know she'll be excited to have it tomorrow."

"Poor thing. Well, at least she's home. That's got to be better than having her in that hospital. And I'm sure you are glad to be back in an actual bed," she said. "You're probably getting real sleep now."

"You'd think, but actually, I'm getting less sleep now that I'm home," I said. "The bed is nice, obviously, but I'm up a million times a night to check on Amelia."

Tina gave me a sympathetic look as she unloaded the bags of ice cream and sundae toppings onto the kitchen counter. She went to the cabinet and pulled out two bowls, then got out the scoop.

"That must be rough. I can't even imagine how worried you must be about her," she said. "I guess that would make it hard to get any good sleep."

"Well, it isn't just that."

Tina picked up the first container of ice cream and scooped some out into each of the bowls, then replaced the top and reached for another flavor.

"What do you mean?" she asked.

"Travis met Amelia," I said.

I could probably have given more of a buildup to that. If I had, Tina might not have dropped the container of ice cream and sent the spoons clattering from the counter onto the floor. But I felt like I needed to just let it out. So, there we were.

Tina crouched down to pick up the spoons and set the ice cream back on the counter. By the look on her face when she slowly stood back up, her face appearing from behind the counter as she did, I didn't think she would have even noticed if the entire container had spilled out and spread across the kitchen floor.

"He what?" she asked, her voice dropping to a conspiratorial whisper.

I nodded. "He met her."

Tina's eyes widened, and she scooped the ice cream faster. "Tell me everything." I started to speak, but she cut me off. "Hold on." She finished putting the ice cream in the bowls and then went to my refrigerator, pulling out the bottle of wine she stashed there in case of emergencies. "We're trading up. Come on."

I got new spoons out of the drawer and glasses down from the cabinet, then followed her into the living room.

107

She'd hauled in the bowls of ice cream and the toppings and spread them out on the coffee table. Dropping down on the floor on one side of the table, she pulled a bowl toward her and started covering it with toppings.

"Go ahead."

"When we first got to the hospital, he was the one who initially examined her," I said.

"You didn't tell me that," Tina said, still augmenting her ice cream. At this point she was at a pretty even ratio of ice cream to toppings.

"I know. I didn't want to make a big deal out of it. Amelia was in so much pain she didn't even really remember talking to him, and he didn't say anything to me. But then he came to her room the next morning and told me he knew she was his." I took her lead and started adding to my own ice cream. I then reached for the bottle of wine. "How wrong do you think it would be for me to just pour this over the ice cream and create a float?"

Tina shrugged. "It is a dessert wine."

I looked at the bottle, considering it for a second, then shook my head. "Probably shouldn't." I poured it into a glass instead. "Anyway, we talked, and he said he already knew she was his. He said he wasn't going to fight me for custody, but he didn't say he didn't want to know her or anything. Then he showed up in the room again when she was awake and had me introduce them."

"Did you tell Amelia who he is?" Tina asked through a massive bite of her ice cream.

"No," I told her. "I thought she already had enough going on, and that when I did tell her, it should be in a different situation."

"I completely agree. That's a lot for her to take in. What are you going to do?"

"Call my best friend and beg for advice."

"That's a good idea," Tina said. She took another bite of ice cream, then threw her hands up in the air, widening her eyes like she was surprised. "Would you look at that. Here I am."

I laughed. "Convenient how things worked out like that." The humor left me quickly. "I really don't know what to do."

"I know. Let's just talk this out."

We talked for a while, going over everything that happened and working through different scenarios. But no matter how many different ways we tried to talk about it, it always came back to the same conclusion of what I needed to do next: talk to Travis and figure out what kind of relationship he wanted with our daughter, if any.

Later that night after Tina left, I still couldn't stop thinking about Travis. My mind left the thoughts of seeing him in the hospital and the confusion of what I was supposed to do now and wandered back to the time we spent together.

Images of the steamy nights I spent with him overtook me, and my hand traveled down my body until my fingers worked to mimic the same incredible way he used to make me feel.

CHAPTER 17

TRAVIS

Hank sat in his easy chair, his fingers steepled and his chin resting on them. The slight beer gut had become a table for his bag of chips, and a soda pop sat on the actual table beside him. I eyed him, trying to see if I could gauge his true feelings about the matter before he tried to sugarcoat them into words, but he was cagey. He just sat, staring down at his raised feet on the reclined chair, and took a moment to compose his words. Finally, his eyes flicked over to mine, and he straightened up.

"You know, I've known you all your life, Travis," he said.

"I know."

"And in all that time, I always knew you would be someone who would rise above. Someone who would be better than their upbringing. I think that's why your daddy kind of left you alone, you know? He knew you were going to be okay. He didn't want to get in the way of the man you were becoming," Hank said. "I know you have issues with who your mom and dad were to you. I get that. I even understand it and even though I stood up for him before, I

agree with you. They weren't cut out to be parents. But you are your own man."

I nodded.

"I can just feel the whole town judging me," I said.

"Fuck the town," Hank said, and the bluntness startled me so much I instinctively laughed.

"What?"

"Who cares what they think of you," Hank said. "You don't have to let anybody else tell you who you are. My advice is to ignore them."

There was a moment of silence while I took that in. It might sound good, but simply not caring wasn't exactly in my wheelhouse. The only thing that ever seemed to help me not care about what other people thought was the primary reason I had a sponsor. It had led me to some dark places.

"I see what you're saying, but I've spent my whole life trying to prove I'm not just 'the drunk's kid' that I don't even know how to not think of *myself* that way. It literally defines who I am," I said. "How do I get past that?"

"I don't know, kid," Hank said, digging through the chips to find one he liked and popping it into his mouth. "All I know is that you have to find a way. You can't spend your whole life trying to please everybody. If you do, you end up a lonely, miserable old man eating cold beans out of a can."

"I guess," I muttered.

"Shoot," Hank said. "You are young and smart and in a profession where you are going to end up wealthy. And now you find out you have a baby girl with the lady you still are in love with? And she's still single? Son, I'd do a lot of things just to have the problems you've got."

I stayed for a little while longer, but enlightenment was

just not to be. As much as it seemed that Hank wanted the best for me and genuinely cared for me, in spite of my outburst at the diner, he didn't seem to have any wise input the way I had hoped. It felt unfair that I didn't have the classic father figure to go to for advice, and I lamented that as I got into my car and headed back home. Though much of our time was spent without much usable advice, his insistence that I couldn't spend my life trying to please other people still rolled over in my mind as I tucked in to get an early night's sleep.

Monday arrived and I still hadn't heard from Carrie. I was starting to believe I never would, unless of course I pushed the subject. I understood why she didn't tell me at first, but at this point the cat was out of the bag. I knew. I had met little Amelia and had spoken to her. She knew my face. Waiting for Carrie to make the first move was legitimate torture.

I was wound up in the idea of getting to know Amelia better. It shouldn't have surprised me, but it did anyway. I never saw myself falling into a profession of helping children, and yet I did. I never saw myself as a father, and yet I was. Turned out, I wasn't all that great at predicting my own future.

Still, Amelia was a whole person already. The days of being a baby and learning and growing, all that was gone. I'd missed that entire time, and a part of me I knew I should lock away and never address that I was actually upset about it. But even more than that, I wanted to know Amelia now. I didn't want to waste a bunch of time. If we were going to have some sort of relationship, I wanted to get to it.

But that was up to Carrie. I needed to accept her decision. It was my fault I never knew about Amelia. I was the one that ignored her calls when she'd found out about her. I was the one who had run away in the first place. I was the culprit of all the problems in this situation, and if I hadn't come back to do my residency, I likely never would have known.

I was mulling over possibly texting her, just to let her know that I was available to talk when I heard my name over the loudspeaker. I looked up curiously as the message was read out. I had a visitor at the front desk. Had Hank finally stumbled on some sage wisdom he wanted to impart?

"Sounds like you need a break," Dr. Jones said, taking the clipboard out of my hand. "Why don't you take your lunch? I can handle this."

"Are you sure?" I asked. Dr. Jones got a weary smile on his face, and I recognized the sarcasm before he even spoke.

"Oh, I think I might be able to manage. I only have twenty some odd years' experience. I'll be sure to call if I get tripped up."

"Very funny, sir," I said.

I rolled my eyes as the real, genuine grin began to spread across his face.

"Thanks Doc," I said. "I'll be back in a few minutes."

"Do hurry," Dr. Jones said, going back to the clipboard. "I might get lost in the catacombs of the hospital. Doddering old man that I am."

He cackled to himself as I walked away.

As I neared the front desk, I cocked my head to the side when Carrie standing there, and I nearly stopped in my tracks. She was staring back at me, an expression I couldn't read on her face and in her eyes. I tried to control my breathing as I made it closer to her, forcing out a smile.

"Hi, Carrie."

"Hey," she said.

Something in her voice told me that the conversation we

were about to have wasn't going to be terribly pleasant. A part of me wanted to tell her I couldn't talk and that I would have to meet her some other time, somewhere other than work. And we could discuss things then. Instead, I just swallowed the words that were bubbling up, forcing them down and accepting that whatever happened next, at least it would answer a few questions that had kept me up the last couple of nights.

"Do you want to talk? I have an hour or so for lunch," I asked.

"That would be great," she said. "I don't want to keep you."

I shook my head. "No, it's fine, I brought lunch with me today. We can go out to the picnic tables and talk. It's unseasonably warm today."

"Sure."

I ran into the breakroom and grabbed my lunch from the refrigerator, glad that I had stopped by the grocery store on Sunday to grab what I needed. A nice chicken Caesar salad while talking to Carrie would be a million times better than yet another turkey sub. And I'd had my fill of sushi for the next six months, especially store-bought, middle-of-Wisconsin sushi.

We headed outside into the weirdly warm early afternoon. Carrie was wrapped up in a coat which she quickly shed when we got to the picnic table, while I kept on my light jacket. She sat down across from me at the table, and I pulled out my salad, grabbing a bite as I searched for the words.

"So," I began.

"So," she repeated. Apparently neither one of us wanted to start the conversation, but I was determined to let her go first. I didn't want to be the one to assume what the relationship was going to be. Not for me and her, and not for me and Amelia. She deserved me backing off and setting the boundaries.

The last thing I wanted to happen was for her to think I'd come here to mess up her life. Those words were right there on the edge of my tongue, and I wanted to spit them out, to get them into her head and clear the air. I was sure that once she realized I wasn't here to hurt her, or to screw things up for her, she would feel much more at ease. Then the business of what was going to happen from this point forward would be much more amiable.

But I couldn't make the words come out. Fear locked them in my throat, and I ended up just watching as her eyes scanned the parking lot and the trees beyond. Not far from the direction she was looking was my apartment. Where I lived, yet again in Monroe. A place I promised I never would be again, not without her. And I had no reason to think I would ever have her again.

Yet, here she was, at the picnic table, no ring on her finger and there to discuss our daughter. A link that would keep us connected forever.

I was pretty sure I knew how the conversation was about to go. Her grim expression told me almost everything. She was going to turn to me and tell me that she believed I would be a bad influence. And she didn't want me to be around our kid, and that she thought I would just screw her up. And it was going to be hard enough to avoid the genetics of my parents in her without my interference, adding it would just put her behind the eight ball her entire life.

She would just want to move on like she never saw me. Pretend it never happened, we keep our space, and maybe I could send money every once in a while, to help support her. I knew she would never ask for it, but I would offer. It was only right. She was still my daughter and helping her was something I could do even if Carrie didn't want me to know her at all.

This is why I was so surprised, so dumbfounded when she turned to me and said what she said. It was so far out of my thoughts of what she could possibly want to talk about or say to me that I dropped a piece of chicken off the fork, bouncing off the container and landing in the grass for the birds to get later.

"Why did you leave me?" she asked.

And the breath went out of my lungs.

CHAPTER 18

CARRIE

I t was not how I'd intended this conversation to start.
Tina agreed to take care of Amelia so I could come
have this talk with Travis, and I had thought I was ready. I
went over what I was going to say and came to terms with
what I thought I wanted before even leaving the house.

This conversation was going to be about him getting to
know his daughter in a safe, controlled, and healthy way
that put her needs and reactions as the top priority. We
would talk about the best way to tell her that Travis wasn't
just a friend of mine who was nice enough to help take care
of her at the hospital but was actually her father. Then we'd
decide how to schedule time for them to spend together so
they could get to know each other.

I felt confident I had it in me to handle this. I wasn't the
same girl he left behind. Seven years later, I was an adult
who had gotten stronger and more secure in myself.

At least, that was what I convinced myself of until I was
actually standing face-to-face with him and the only thing
on my mind was what happened all that time ago.

Every bit of preparation went straight to hell, and the

only thing I could get out of my mouth was that question. But in truth, it was the most important question. None of this would be happening, we wouldn't be here like this, if that moment in time hadn't happened. And I wanted to know what led to it.

I tried to tell myself it had something to do with how I would integrate him into Amelia's life, but I knew that wasn't really the case. I'd been wondering what had happened to make him walk away before I even knew Amelia was coming. It wasn't just about her. It was about me too.

Even after all the years apart, I knew Travis well. I understood his emotions and could read even the slightest changes in his features, which was why it took me aback slightly when I saw heartbreak cross his face. I didn't think he felt that way. After all, he was the one who left me. He was the one who walked out of my life without a single word and hadn't made any effort to contact me since.

Part of me wanted to lash out at him for it, but I stopped myself. If I was ever going to get answers to the questions I had been carrying for the last seven years, I had to be willing to hear him out.

"Things were going so well with us before college. I thought it would always be that way. That no matter what, we would get through anything together. I couldn't imagine anything that would get in our way or keep us apart," Travis said.

His voice was shaky, halting as he spoke. It was like the words had been locked up inside of him for so long they didn't want to come out, but he was forcing them. I nodded.

"I know. That was how I felt too. I really believed there was nothing that could ever change how we felt about each other. But then things got rough. We weren't seeing each other as much. We weren't talking as much."

"We were busy," I said. "School. Work. Projects. Things were taking up a lot of time. But that didn't mean I didn't miss you or want to be with you. I don't understand why you just left. I know you came by the night before you left. My dad said you were drunk. Why? Were you coming to break up with me?"

"No, I wasn't. I didn't want to lose you, but I still felt you slipping away a bit. I wanted to see you. So, I went to your parents' house. It was late, but I just needed to talk to you. I just needed to see you for a second and know everything was okay. I was drunk, and when I showed up, your father came to the door. He knew I was a mess and completely ripped me apart. He told me I wasn't good enough for you and that I was screwing up your life.

"And the thing was, I knew he was right. As soon as he said it, it made me realize what I was doing. I was spiraling completely out of control, and I was going to take you down with me. You didn't deserve that. You had your whole amazing life ahead of you, and I was just going to be in your way. I wasn't good enough for you. So, I left," he said.

I was stunned. I knew he had been there. I could remember hearing his voice and waking up thinking it had been a dream. I even knew my father had spoken to him and that he'd been drunk. But I didn't understand the extent. I didn't know just how horrible my father had been to him. I was pissed as hell at him not only for making it his place to do that, but for keeping it from me for all these years.

But it wasn't just my father. I was angry at Travis too. He didn't have to run. He didn't have to just accept what my father had said and leave me behind. I shook my head.

"So, that's just it?" I asked.

Travis looked at me with an expression that was surprised and slightly stunned.

"What do you mean?" he asked.

"That's just it?" I repeated. "My father says those things to you, and you just go? Why didn't you fight for me? Did I really mean that little to you?"

"You meant everything to me, Carrie. That's the thing. Weren't you listening?" he asked.

"I was listening enough to hear you say that my father told you we weren't good together, and you just took that at face value."

"No," Travis said firmly. "Your father didn't say you and I weren't good together. He said I wasn't good for you. That I was ruining your life."

"And you just accepted it. You didn't even blink. You just turned and walked away from me rather than fighting or standing up for us," I said.

"In the condition I was in right then, your father was absolutely right. I was drinking constantly. I was going out of my mind. I was willing to drive over to your house drunk in the middle of the night. That kind of self-destructive bullshit wasn't what you needed in your life. You're better than that. You should want better than that."

"What I wanted was you," I fired back. "And when you were gone, I at least wanted to know what happened. Why you were so willing to turn your back on me and everything we shared. But I never got that. You never told me what was going on or reached out to me. I had to just keep wondering," I said.

"I figured you would just put me behind you, forget me, and move on."

"There's no way I could forget what we had," I said. "You were my life. My future. I thought you loved me.

Then you were just gone. And even if it wasn't for that, I couldn't forget when I was carrying your child." He glanced away, and I drew in a breath that shook slightly in my lungs and ached in my throat. "Would you have stayed?"

"What do you mean?" he asked.

"If you had known I was pregnant before that night, would you have stayed?" I asked.

"Carrie," Travis said like he couldn't believe I was asking that question.

"I need to know."

He let out a breath, and his head shook back and forth slowly. My stomach sank. "I can't tell you honestly. That doesn't mean I absolutely wouldn't have, or that I can't see myself wanting to stay. That isn't it at all. I don't know what I would have done at twenty. I was already scared of turning into my father and proving the town right. As much as I would have wanted to be there for my baby, I don't know if I would have been able to face the fear of messing up and proving that everybody was right about their perception of me."

"So, you would have left anyway," I said.

"I said I don't know how I would have reacted."

I wanted to walk away. I came here to talk about him getting to know Amelia, but the conversation was going in a completely different direction. The only thing that kept me there was the look of sadness in his eyes. I drew in a breath.

"Do you want to know your daughter now?" I asked. "More than just saying hello to her in a hospital room?"

"Yes," Travis said without hesitation. "I want to be a part of her life."

"What about when your residency is over?" I asked. "You have to understand she's just a little girl. She has grown up her entire life without a father, but she's been asking. She wants to know who you are and to have you be a part of her life. That's not just something you can take casually. You coming into her life would be a major change for her, but if you were just suddenly gone, it would be devastating. You can't just have a relationship with her for three years and then leave when it's over and expect that to be okay."

"I know that," Travis said.

"Then what are you going to do when the three years is over? You've already said you didn't plan on staying here when you're done with your residency. So, what happens now?" I asked.

"Honestly, I haven't thought that far ahead yet. This is all a really big deal to me too, Carrie. This is changing my life too. You can't expect me to be able to just take it all in and instantly know what to think and feel or what I'm going to do next. Right now, I can tell you I want to have a relationship with her. I want to get to know her and be a part of her life," he said.

I nodded, trying to wrap my head around everything he said, but I couldn't. I looked at the time. "I've got to go. Tina is taking care of Amelia right now, but I don't want to be away from her for too long."

"I have to get back to work anyway," Travis said. "Let me know what we're going to do next."

I agreed and left, feeling even more conflicted than I did at the start of it all.

CHAPTER 19

TRAVIS

Most days, my dreams were like half-lucid nightmares. Not the terrifying ones where I would find myself kidnapped or hurt in some way. Not in the falling off a cliff or out of a plane sort of thing either. No. Most of the time my dreams involved the anxieties and fears I had growing up and becoming the person I had turned into since leaving Monroe.

All too often, I would wake up in a cold sweat, memories of my past so vivid and present that I could feel the burn of the smoke of my father's cigarette in my nostrils or taste the stale leftover macaroni on the back of my tongue. So many times I woke as a child to an empty house. Many other times I woke to a house that may as well have been empty. My parents might have been there, but they weren't really there. Passed out on the floor of the living room or on their bed, a bottle of whatever they had been drinking sometimes spilled where they'd fallen asleep was often how I found them.

One recurring dream was a memory that I was helpless to change. I knew it was a memory but was stuck, watching it happen again and again through my tiny child eyes. I was seven. Mom had just started to get really bad then. Before, she used to wake me up, get me dressed, and make my breakfast. Then breakfast became me making my own cereal while she sat at the table rubbing her head and taking Tylenol. Then it was just waking me up, motioning to a laundry basket with my clothes in it unfolded and grunting as she went to bed.

But that morning, I woke on my own. The cat clock I had in the corner, some cartoon I didn't recognize but was apparently funny to Mom, read that it was already ten in the morning. I knew I'd missed my bus. It would have come some time ago. But if I got dressed and ready, Mom or Dad could take me to school. At least at school all of the lights in the building worked and I got a hot lunch.

I wondered if maybe that day was an off day, but it wasn't. I realized quickly what had happened when I walked into the kitchen and found Mom, sound asleep on the tile, a bottle of brown alcohol I knew now was whiskey in her hand. I had shrugged, gone back into my room and turned on my TV. She would wake up eventually.

Those were the dreams I had usually. But recently, those dreams had given me a break. A much needed one at that, although I wasn't sure the dreams I was having were much better. Now my dreams were of a much more recent past. A past that still seemed tangible and changeable. A past that was so close I could still feel the fabric on the tips of my fingers, and when I woke from them, I groaned that they weren't true.

This morning, I woke groaning again. Desperately, I smacked at the alarm on my phone, hoping if I held my eyes shut, if I tried to stay in that weird fugue state between awake and asleep, I could go back there for just a little bit more time. For a moment it worked. I was back. I was eighteen. And I was with Carrie.

She was wearing the red plaid skirt she knew I liked, and her lips were sparkling with the baby pink lip gloss. I had snuck over in the middle of the night, but she knew I was on my way. We had talked about it all day. Her father was on a business trip, and her mother slept like the dead when he wasn't around. Carrie's room was on another floor of the house, and the chances of anyone noticing me were small if I were careful.

I had climbed up the side of the porch like a ninja. I had done it so many times it was automatic to me. The dim light from the streetlamp across from her house gave me enough to see by, but I didn't need it. I knew how to get there, and I knew where to place my feet. I had crawled through her open window and saw her sitting on her bed in the candlelight.

The outfit was one I told her I liked offhandedly one day, and she wore it whenever she could. She was so incredibly sexy, and the long socks that went past her knees highlighted her tight thighs. I moved to her quickly, and our lips crushed into each other. My hands roamed her body, sliding into the white button-up shirt to play with her breasts. She didn't wear a bra with that outfit. Or panties.

My cock was stiff in an instant, and her lips parted as she kissed down the center of my chest. I gripped her hair as she unzipped my pants and her hand wrapped around my staff. She stroked me, and her tongue slid around the tip.

And the alarm went off again.

I sighed as I opened my eyes and hit the snooze again. There was no going back to sleep now. Not with my cock standing at full attention as it was. Feeling guilty about it, I reached down and let my hand wrap around my cock as I closed my eyes. Her face came back to me instantly, as did the memory of the way she looked when she climaxed. The way her lips curled into an 'O' shape and her breasts bounced while I pounded into her. I released in the bed to the memory and then groaned as I realized I barely had time for a shower before work.

Still, it was worth it.

When work finally wound down, I realized I hadn't been able to keep her off my mind the entire time. I felt terrible about it, but my mind kept wandering to those memories and then to the wonder of how she looked now. Now that time had been so kind to her and she had become such a gorgeous adult woman. How would her body feel now? How would her lips feel now?

Those questions haunted me all day, every time I was alone, and when I finally clocked out, I headed home knowing what I was going to do. I was going to call her. I wasn't entirely sure what I was going to say when I heard her on the other end of the line, but I was going to call her anyway.

I tossed the keys into the bowl by the door as soon as I walked in and made it to my bedroom first. Changing into a sweatshirt and some stretchy pajama pants, I went to the kitchen to grab a cold water bottle. Those dreams were making me miss her like crazy, but I needed to maintain my cool if I was going to speak to her in real life. There were a lot of things to talk about, not the least of which was our daughter. If I was going to have a chance to be in her life, I couldn't let my dream memories get in the way of having a normal relationship with Carrie.

"Hello?" she said as she picked up on the other end. I lay back onto the couch and made myself comfortable.

"Hi, Carrie. Is now an okay time to talk?"

There was a little bit of hesitation in her voice, but then she sounded like she walked into another room. I could hear her muffled voice as she pressed the phone to her chest. "Mom, can you watch Amelia for a little bit? I have a call I need to take."

I couldn't hear her Mom's response, but after a little bit more walking sounds, a door shut, and Carrie breathed out as she got back to the phone.

"There we go," she said. "I've got some time."

"You're in the office, aren't you?"

"How did you know?"

"You haven't changed that much, Carrie," I said.

It was true. Ever since we were younger, when I called her and her parents were awake, she would duck into the office her father never actually used. It was set up so he could work from home, but it ended up becoming a glorified homework and craft room. Her mother loved to crochet and would often be found in there. Carrie would take her phone calls in there because she could lock the door, and it was a room separated by the kitchen and the laundry room on either side. Meaning there was usually enough sound not to be eavesdropped on.

"What did you want to talk about?" Carrie asked. "Is this about seeing Amelia?"

"Yes," I said. "I do want to get to know her. I was wondering if it would be alright with you, I would work on making sure I could stay here after my residency."

"Are you sure about that?" The lack of confidence in her voice was telling, but I pushed on.

"Yes," I said firmly. "If you're comfortable with me being in her life, I want to be there for her. I want to be a good father. You... you know why."

There was a sharp inhale of breath on the other end. "I know, Travis."

"Good. We can work out the details later. I know it's getting late."

"It is," she said. "She usually is already in bed by now, but I was running around at the grocery store."

"So, her bedtime is nine?" I asked.

"Is that a criticism?" she asked, attitude suddenly back in her voice.

"No, not at all," I said. "Just trying to get some details about her day-to-day life. Like, if I happened to call and wanted to talk to her, I would have to do it before nine, that sort of thing."

"Oh," she said, taking a moment. "No, her bedtime is usually eight to eight-thirty. She's usually asleep by nine, but I was busy today, and Mom watched a movie with her that she didn't start until seven."

"I'll remember that," I said.

"Okay. Well, good night," Carrie said.

"Good night, Carrie."

As I sat the phone down, I looked around the small apartment. It was free; there was that, but it was also rather small. And as it was, my furniture was cramped into the rooms, and I had already sold a chair online because I had nowhere for it to go.

If I was going to have a little girl, and if I was ever going to be able to have her at my own home, there was going to have to be a few changes. I didn't think I would be able to be alone with Amelia for a good long while, but when I was, I wanted her to feel comfortable and safe. To feel like anything she wanted or needed she could get at my place. I wanted her mother to feel the same way.

The apartment had the upside of being free with my

residency, but that wasn't going to be enough. I was going to have to find somewhere new. Somewhere bigger. Something with a second bedroom.

Briefly, I let myself think about what it would be like to have them both with me. To have Carrie on the couch, reading a book or jotting things down in the notebook she just about always had with her. To have Amelia playing on the floor with her toys while I called for takeout. The three of us, sitting at a dining room table, eating.

Fantasies. No different from the morning and my memories. For right now, I just had to focus on what I could realistically do—that was to be there for my daughter.

CHAPTER 20

CARRIE

The phone call from Travis surprised me. When we ended our conversation, he basically said the ball was in my court and I could decide how we were going to move forward. Then he was the one to call, and suddenly everything felt suddenly more real. It wasn't about me trying to take one step at a time and figure it out anymore. Travis was serious about this and wasn't going to let me take too much time.

He made it clear he wanted to not only meet Amelia but start spending time with her regularly. It was what I thought I wanted from the beginning. It was the whole reason I came out and told Travis about Amelia, wasn't it?

Yet, it felt like it was coming at me so fast, and I was getting overwhelmed thinking about him being around so much. Even though he didn't say it, after our conversation on the phone, I fully expected Travis to take it upon himself to find time to see Amelia. When she was feeling up to going to the bakery, I waited all day for him to show up.

He didn't the first day, but that didn't take away the on edge feeling the second day. As it turned out, I wasn't the only one thinking about him coming to the bakery. When I got home on the third day I was back at the bakery, I got a call from Travis.

"I thought about coming to the bakery today," he said.

"I was actually expecting you to," I said. "Why didn't you?"

"The more I thought about it, the more I realized that wasn't the right way to do this. I don't want to encroach on your space. The bakery is yours, and Amelia should feel totally at ease there, not like I'm just going to spring up out of nowhere. I think it would be better if we planned on meeting in a neutral place."

Relief rushed through me. I was glad to know I didn't have to always be tense, worrying about him just showing up.

"I really appreciate that. Where are you thinking?" I asked.

"Well, I was thinking that park where we used to go. I played there when I was a kid, so maybe she would like it, too."

Memories surfaced in my mind that I hadn't let come up in years. Images of the afternoons Travis and I spent walking along the stone paths together and stealing kisses in the secluded corners of that park flashed through my thoughts. But I made myself push them away and focus on what we were talking about.

"She loves that park. I bring her there all the time in the spring and summer. But it's so cold right now. I don't know if the playground is the best idea," I said.

"It's supposed to snow," Travis said, sounding excited at the prospect. "What's better than playing in the snow? We'll go to the old soccer field. They still don't use that, do they?"

That field hadn't been used for soccer practices and games since I was just a few years older than Amelia. When a big new sports complex portion of the park was built on the other side, the old field turned into a place where families went to picnic, play Frisbee, and fly kites. I always thought that was an improvement. Many summer nights were spent lying on blankets spread on the ground, staring up at the sky and watching the stars.

"It's just like it always was," I tell him.

"Good. Then let's meet there," he said. "Saturday?"

I couldn't help but smile. "We'll see you then."

I thought about our weekend plans for the rest of the week. I didn't really know what to expect. It wasn't just going to the park to play in the snow. It was a huge moment for Amelia and me. Right now, the idea of a father was just that—an idea. It was something she knew she had and something she wanted to know more about. But it was abstract.

This would all change on Saturday. As soon as that official introduction was made, her entire idea of a father would shift. She would know who he was and the process of starting a relationship would begin. But I knew there was a chance it wouldn't go the way we thought and hoped it would.

Maybe they wouldn't get along. Maybe she would be angry I'd misled her at the hospital or upset with Travis. Maybe she would realize that not knowing who her father was gave her the option of fantasizing about him and what it would be like to have one but knowing who he was ended that.

There were a lot of maybes running around in my head, and the anxiety kept building even as I held Amelia's hand and walked with her down the narrow path leading from the parking lot to the field.

The snow had come and coated the ground with several sparkling white inches, and that morning we woke up to new flakes drifting down from the sky. It was beautiful, and I knew Amelia was excited to play, but we needed to get through the big hurdle first.

Travis was already waiting when we got to the field. He was sitting on a bench with a plastic basket beside him. As we got closer, I could see several small snow toys inside. Amelia pointed at him.

"Look, Mama. It's Dr. King," she said.

I nodded. "I know, baby. He's here to meet us."

"Really?"

"Yes."

Travis stood up as we got close and smiled at Amelia.

"Hi," he said. "How are you feeling?"

"Good. Do you like the snow?" she asked.

He smiled a little and nodded. "I do."

I crouched down beside Amelia and put my arm around her. "Honey, remember I told you this morning there was something I needed to tell you?"

"Yes," she said.

"It's about Dr. King. I told you he's an old friend of mine. But he's more than that. You see—" I looked up at Travis, and he drew in a breath, preparing himself for the moment when all our lives would change. "He's your daddy."

I waited for the impact. Part of me expected her to be upset or wary. Instead, her eyes instantly lit up.

"He is?" she asked.

I nodded, and she looked over at Travis, who nodded.

"I am."

Amelia ran over to him with open arms, and Travis

crouched down to accept her hug. Her arms wrapped tightly around his neck, and she buried her face in it.

"I asked Santa for you," she whispered.

Travis's eyes closed, and he held her close, and for an instant my heart both broke and swelled. They clung to each other for a couple of seconds, and then Amelia stepped back, grabbing onto his hand and starting to tug him out into the field.

"I'll just sit here," I said, pointing to the bench. "You guys have a good time."

Even though it was so cold sitting there on the freezing bench, I wouldn't give up a second of watching the two of them talk and play in the snow together.

They played for as long as I felt comfortable with Amelia being out there, making snow angels and building snowmen they decorated with some of the toys Travis brought. They both looked disappointed when I told them it was time to go and were already making plans for their next get-together.

But their next meeting happened the next afternoon. On Monday we got together for dinner at one of Amelia's favorite restaurants, then went for ice cream. I was feeling good right up until I got home and found my parents sitting at my kitchen island with tea.

"Come on in," I said dryly when I walked in to put away the extra ice cream Travis bought for Amelia. "Make yourself a cup of tea."

"Where have you been?" Dad asked.

I looked around. "I'm sorry. Did I just go back in time? Because I thought I was an adult who lives in my own home."

"You don't need to be rude," Mom said. "We were just worried when we called and you didn't answer."

"So, you decided to take it upon yourself to come in and wait for me?"

"Hi, Grandma, hi, Grandpa," Amelia said, running into the room and climbing into my mother's lap. "We went for dinner and ice cream with my daddy."

"Oh, did you?" Mom said, looking over at me.

"Yep. It was really fun. He likes Rocky Road too. Maybe that's why I like it," she said.

"Maybe," Dad said.

"Honey, go on and get ready for your bath. I'll be up in just a little bit to add the bubbles," I said.

"Okay," Amelia said, scrambling down from Mom's lap. She kissed each of her grandparents and ran toward her bedroom.

"The two of you are spending a lot of time with him," Dad said.

"He's her father," I reminded him. "They're getting to know each other."

"Don't you think it's too much, too soon?"

"It does seem like you just jumped into things," Mom said.

"Jumped into things?" I asked incredulously. "She's six years old."

"You just want to make sure that you're protecting her and that everything is going to work out."

"What's that supposed to mean?"

"I don't want her getting too attached and then something goes wrong. You already know how this went once. You could be setting her up for some real heartbreak," Dad said.

I let out an exasperated sigh. "Thank you so much for your support."

"You don't need to get defensive," Mom said.

"You know what? Yes, I do. Because if you haven't noticed, that little girl in there is elated. She has been asking about her father, and now finally she has him. And he's been amazing with her. They are getting to know each other and forming a relationship that, frankly, both of them have deserved for the last seven years," I said angrily.

"She does look happy," Mom said. "And we're not discounting that."

"Her being happy is the most important thing," Dad added.

"Then let it be. Stop trying to turn it into what it isn't." My eyes slid over to my father. "You already destroyed what I had with Travis. Don't do the same thing to your grand-daughter. I'm going to get her ready for bed. You can see yourselves out."

I walked out of the room without another word. I wasn't going to let them ruin the sheer happiness Amelia was feeling. She and Travis were getting along and having fun together. Things weren't perfect, and there were still some difficult moments and awkwardness we were working our way through. She was still asking questions about why it took so long for him to come around and why we weren't a real family, but she was also so happy. This was what mattered right then. We could get to the rest as time went along.

It wasn't just about Amelia. Watching Travis around our child was making me remember all our good times. And there were so many of those. The years we spent together were wonderful, and most of the best moments of my life had him in them.

He had definitely grown. I could see how much time had changed him, in all the best ways. He was surer of himself now, and he didn't seem to have the same trouble and struggles he did then. The best part was seeing how sweet he was with Amelia.

I honestly wasn't expecting that. It wasn't that he wasn't sweet to me because he always was. I just thought the years would have hardened him, and not knowing her might have made him hesitant. But he wasn't. He settled right into his role with her and seemed to light up around her.

I was a bit angry at myself for doubting him. I should have known the man I once loved so much would be good with his daughter. But watching them together made me long for the actual family we could have been if it weren't for him leaving.

CHAPTER 21

TRAVIS

The last few days had been amazing. Getting to know Amelia was a slow process and one that was not going to be rushed. But every time I saw her, she warmed up to me more and more. It was exciting and fun to see her point of view of life and the things that were happening around her. I marveled at how smart and precocious she was and how often things she did or said reminded me of myself. I'd had no influence on her up until just the past few days, and yet there were times where genetics raised its head and showed up. There was no doubt that she was a perfect mixture of her mother and myself, and I felt myself sinking deeply into the joy of being around her.

Also, being around Carrie as an adult was eye-opening and making me even more regretful of how I'd acted years ago. But, while I could mope and wish I could take it all back every day, instead I was just enjoying the time around her. She was funny and silly with our daughter in ways I remembered but were still different. The years that passed between us had matured her, in all the best ways. She was a mom, sure, but the life and energy that drew me to her when we were younger was still there. Even amplified. It was as if giving birth had only taken that energy and doubled it.

Work was long and stressful but thinking about the growing relationship between my daughter and Carrie and I was helping me get through it. Those thoughts carried me through hours on my feet and the learning curve of working in a fast-paced environment produced. Usually, when things got tough, and I had too much on my plate, the default was to think about getting a drink. It was the self-destructive behavior that led to me making call after call to my sponsor. But in these last few days, I noticed I hadn't had a thought about drinking at all.

It would have been a miracle if I didn't have everything else hanging over my head. Namely, Carrie's parents and how they felt about me being involved in Amelia's life. It was complicated with them, because according to Carrie, they might have accepted that I had matured. They just still had a problem with me, period. It was somewhat under-standable, and as I stood outside of her parents' house, I tried to remind myself of that fact.

But I was still determined. Carrie was standing next to me and had come up with the idea. Amelia was hanging out with Tina so there were no distractions. I took a deep breath.

"You don't have to do this, you know," she said.

"I know, but I'm going to," I said. "This is the deal."

The door opened and Mrs. Jacobs stood in the doorway, a hint of a smile on her face. She had always seemed warmer to me than Carrie's father. He was surly and rude to me at every turn. Mrs. Jacobs, on the other hand, had more softness in her eyes and voice when she spoke to me.

"Hello, Travis," she said, then turned to Carrie. "Hi, baby. Come on in."

I followed Carrie inside and was stunned to see the room looked exactly like it had the last time I saw it. The living room stretched long into the dining room area, and the kitchen was just off to the side of that. The furniture, brown and white and ancient, sat in their normal positions, exactly as they were the last time I had been there. Mr. Jacobs sat in his easy chair reading a book, feet propped up. He had a belly now that he didn't have when I lived in Monroe last, but otherwise, the only change was a smattering of grey in the hair at his temples.

Mrs. Jacobs sat down on the couch in the corner closest to her husband, and Carrie took a seat beside her on the other end. I sat in the chair beside that closest to Carrie, and there was a moment of awkward silence. Finally, Mrs. Jacobs clapped her hands on her thighs and turned sharply to me.

"Would you like something to drink?" she asked. Mr. Jacobs's eyes darted over to me to see how I would react. It was a test. Or a dig. Maybe both.

"Water, please," I said.

"Do you have any wine?" Carrie asked.

"Sure," Mrs. Jacobs said, then turned back to me. "Water?"

I nodded. "Yes, thank you."

A prim smile crossed her face as she walked away toward the kitchen. We sat there quietly with her father continuing to read, or at least pretending to, while we waited. When Mrs. Jacobs returned, I took my glass and drank about half of it in one gulp. I was nervous, in spite of everything, and it manifested into thirst. Suddenly, Mr. Jacobs put his book down on his lap and turned to us.

"So, you're a doctor now?" Mr. Jacobs said, his eyes looking at me over the rim of his glasses.

"I am," I said. "I'm doing my residency in pediatrics now."

"In Monroe?" he said. "I thought Carrie said you had moved to the East Coast?"

"I did," I said. "But this was the first available residency in the school's network. It just so happened to be where I grew up, so they figured it would be a natural fit for me here."

"Mmm-hmm," Mr. Jacobs said in that way that made it seem like he didn't quite believe it. "So what are you doing for money?"

"Dad," Carrie said.

"It's okay," I said. "It's a valid question."

"No, it's not okay," Carrie said. "Dad, you are being rude."

"I'm being rude?" he asked in that tone that never leads to a productive conversation. I knew it well. It was how he responded to any criticism of himself when he was sitting in judgment of others. "What about leaving you high and dry while you were pregnant?"

"Come on now," Mrs. Jacobs said, but it was too late. Carrie had already taken down her entire glass of wine.

"Maybe he wouldn't have left if you didn't give him the idea," Carrie spat.

"What are you talking about?" he said, suddenly standing, smashing the legs of the reclining chair back. Carrie stood up too, and I found myself on my own feet, close to her.

"He told me how you told him he should leave me alone. That he was no good. That he was ruining my life. You should be ashamed of yourself for telling him that and never even telling me you did it!" Carrie yelled. I could see her hands shaking in anger, and her father took another step toward her. I didn't think he would do something as stupid as hit her, but my past experiences with him wouldn't fade away either. I remember the implicit threat he'd made to me on more than one occasion.

"Well," he said, clearly not know where to go with it, "it was true, dammit! He might have made something of himself now, but that's probably because I told him the truth. He was going to ruin your life."

"Did he?" Carrie asked. "Is that what you think of Amelia? That he ruined my life by giving me her? That she is evidence of my life in ruins?"

"Of course not," he said as I took another step closer to her. Suddenly, he looked old, defeated, and sad. His eyes searched his daughter's face for obedience, and there was none.

"That's the only thing I can think of when you say he would ruin my life, Dad. That he would knock me up. Is that what you were worried about? That you would have a pregnant daughter? That his genes would sully our family line? Is that what you think of Amelia?"

"No," he said, plainly. His eyes had dropped from hers, though. He was searching the ground now, as if in disbelief.

"Then what? Did you think so little of him, so little of me, that you thought he would, what, get me onto drugs? Is that it? Did you think he was going to turn me into a drug addict?" Carrie continued.

"Of course not," he said, but his voice was weaker still.

"Then what?" Carrie yelled. "What was it? What was so wrong with him that you couldn't abide us being together? That you not only told him to go away but then didn't bother to tell me how much of a part you played in him not being here for Amelia? How could you?"

There was silence in the room for a few moments as Carrie struggled to get herself under control. She shoved her arms across her chest and waited. When her father didn't respond, I put my hand on her elbow.

"Maybe I should just go," I offered.

"No," she said. "No, you've appeased them enough already."

"Carrie," her father started. "Just listen to me for a moment. He was... you know his parents."

He left the thought unfinished. It lingered in the air, and the stench of his thought was seen on both Carrie's and her mother's faces. Her mother shook her head and sighed. She was standing in nearly the exact same pose as Carrie, and the resemblance was striking.

"Travis is not his parents," Carrie nearly spat. "He is his own man. He's made mistakes. But he deserves to be judged on his own mistakes and not those of his parents." Again, there was a moment of silence. Mr. Jacobs sat down heavily on the arm of his chair. His expression was one of confusion mixed with anger and disbelief. But there was something else there too. Something almost like regret.

I wasn't going to jump to any conclusions, though.

"Whatever you feel," Carrie continued, "we need to get past it. All of us. Everybody needs to figure their own self out and move forward." She turned her attention directly to her father. "Because Travis is here, and he's staying. Amelia deserves to have her dad be in her life."

Her father sat on the leg of his chair, shocked. I felt shocked too, but I knew I shouldn't have been. The way she had been speaking told me everything I needed to know, in case the last few days spending time with them hadn't already. She was going to give me a chance. A chance to be a good father to Amelia, and a chance to maybe repair some of the damage done between us. I wasn't sure if it would lead to anything romantic, but the spark of hope was there.

She turned to me and offered a weak smile. I returned it. Even in the face of her father's wrath, she had stood up for me. No one else ever had. In that moment I was determined, more than ever, to pay that faith back.

CHAPTER 22

CARRIE

I was still buzzing with adrenaline when Travis and I left my parents' house. The argument had revved me up so much even the calmer conversation after hadn't brought me all the way down. I was glad that conversation happened. It was honest and straightforward, which was exactly what it needed to be. It was a conversation that was seven years in the making. Maybe even longer.

We talked about Amelia and Travis's ongoing role in her life, but we could really be talking about Travis and our relationship when we were younger. It was no secret they didn't want us together then, but we didn't talk about it.

Rather than arguing or trying to push back against them, we just kept going. We pushed through and didn't acknowledge the tension. It seemed like the right thing to do at the time. It seemed like if we just kept our heads down and didn't fight back, we'd be able to ease through the years before we'd be able to be together on our own.

Looking back now, I realized that wasn't the right way to go. We should have stood up for ourselves then. For us. If we had, maybe we would have never gotten to the place where my father could wedge himself between us the way he did. Maybe none of this would have ever happened.

It was good to get everything out in the open now. I loved my parents, and I hated the anger I held for them. This was the first step in really making it go away, and I was glad for that. I was ready for all of this to be over.

Now that I was a mother, I thought I had at least somewhat of a better perspective on what my father did. I could never imagine stepping in and interfering the way he did, but I could appreciate the desire to protect my child. If I thought someone was hurting Amelia or stopping her from doing what she should in life, I would want to guard her. My parents just took it too far.

I understood they did what they thought was right, but it was what led to this mess in the first place, and that was hard to accept.

The energy coursing through me was one I hadn't felt in a while. It reached every part of me, tingling and feeling awake and alive like I hadn't in so long. I stole a look at Travis across the console of the car. My mouth watered, and my stomach quivered. The energy had shifted from adrenaline and anger from the fight with my parents to something else.

I knew exactly what it had become, but I didn't know if it was worth going there. I fought against myself for years to get over Travis. I learned not think about him this way. I struggled with putting those powerful feelings behind me and not letting them control me anymore.

Giving in to the craving I had for him now could just make things much more complicated and confusing. I had to try to ignore it. I just needed to get home and let myself calm down so I could clear my head.

The will to resist didn't last very long.

Travis brought me back to my place and pulled up into the driveway. I gave it only a second after the car stopped to give in to the want that had never really gone away. Getting out of my seat belt, I leaned across the car and kissed him.

It was just a slight kiss at first. More an experiment, an introduction, than anything. I pulled back and lifted my eyes to his, searching his expression for any sign of what he was thinking and feeling. I needed to know his reaction.

I didn't have to wait long. Travis's hand slid up along the side of my face, cupping my cheek and guiding my head forward to bring our mouths together again. We sat there in the car, our mouths playing across each other, our tongues tangling for a few minutes before taking them apart only long enough to scramble out of the car.

We met at the front of the car, and his mouth crushed down on mine again. I didn't know exactly how we did it, but we managed to maneuver to the front door with our mouths barely parting. Travis holding me from behind and kissing along the side of my neck, I unlocked the front door and we got inside.

Within seconds we were fighting off clothes and dragging each other down the hall to my bedroom. I knew I might regret it later, but right then I just wanted to feel him inside me again. It had been so damn long.

He shut the door behind him, and I ran to the bed, jumping onto it and turning on my hands and knees to watch him. The last few months I had spent so much time at my parents' during the holidays that being in my own place was almost like being away in a hotel. It was cool and clean and almost unfamiliar and being there with Travis sent a thrill up my spine that almost made me squeal. I didn't want to think about the ramifications of what we were about to do. I didn't want to think about what this would say about our relationship. I just wanted Travis. In my bed. With me.

He walked slowly through the darkened room, only the light from the window to illuminate it. He began to pull at the buttons of his shirt on his wrist and then the top button near his neck. I waited for him to reach me, and when he was at the edge of the bed, I stood on my knees and pressed my lips into his again. My hands slid down his chest to find the next button that needed to be undone and worked on it. Meanwhile, his hands went to my waist, rising up under my shirt and lifting it until I had to break our embrace so he could yank it off me and toss it away.

Our kiss resumed, and I finished the buttons of his shirt and pushed it off his shoulders. He was wearing a cotton undershirt, and I pulled eagerly at it to get it to untuck from his pants. I felt the pressure of my bra loosen and his fingers run across the freshly nude skin on my back. I pulled my shoulders together to let the bra fall off and away, and Travis immediately filled his palms with my breasts.

I gasped as he moved his lips to my neck, and I pulled his shirt until it came off him too. Not wasting time, I shoved my hand down into the front of his pants, my thumb and forefinger finding his straining cock and grasping it. With my other hand, I undid his belt and button, all while stroking him as best I could in the confined space. He groaned deeply, his lips so close to my ear that the breathy grumble sent goosebumps along my skin. He kneaded my breasts and continued to kiss down to my shoulders as I undid his pants and pulled them down. His boxers were next, and when they finally reached past his hips, his massive, hard cock sprung out of them.

I ran my palm along the length of him, remembering

and experiencing him again as if for the first time all at once. I hadn't been with anyone else since he left, and his touch spoiled me for other men anyway. I couldn't imagine a better lover than the one in my memories, and I longed for it again. I leaned back a bit, still stroking his long staff while his lips moved down my chest and gathered one of my nipples into them. His tongue flicked the tip and brought it to a hard, wet peak and then slid across my chest to do the same to the other. I gasped as the cool air brushed over the wet, pink nipple and then pulled him into me.

Our lips crushed against one another again, and the warmth of his bare chest against mine felt soothing and exciting. He warmed me up and made me hot at the same time, and I quickly moved my lips across his cheek and down his chest. His muscles were bulging, bigger than I remembered them. The time had done him favors, along with what must have been rigorous exercise. Rock-hard abdomen muscles tensed as I made my way down them until my lips were brushing through the tuft of dark mane around his throbbing cock.

Travis groaned as I flicked my tongue along the bottom of his shaft and slid it to the tip. Gathering up the sweet juices there, I swirled around his head, teasing him for just a moment before plunging down and taking him deeply into my mouth. He throbbed and strained against the back wall of my throat as I forced my lips as close to his stomach as I could go. Then, sliding back, I curled my tongue around him underneath and felt him shiver in my touch.

Grinning as I released him from my lips, I grasped his cock at the base and ran my palm up the now slick rod until I reached the tip and twisted gently before plunging it down again. My eyes locked onto his, and he shifted a step forward so that I was pulling him into my breasts. Rubbing the sensitive head against my wet nipples seemed to bring him even more pleasure, and I found myself dying to hear those sounds.

I slid him between my breasts for a moment, pressing them together, and he rocked his hips into me. Flicking out my tongue to lick him as he rose above my pillowy mounds and then dove back again, I felt the heat between my thighs broil. Releasing my breasts, I took him fully into my mouth again and reached down to unbutton my jeans. I slid them down over my ass, yanking at the black cotton panties until they came as well, and shuffled my knees until I could get them all off. Naked, I sucked him for a few moments more, letting him rock his hips and hold my head in place.

Suddenly, he pulled away and bent down to press his lips to mine. I reached for his cock, but he had pulled it way. I opened my eyes to look into his, and he grinned.

"My turn," he grumbled. "Stay there."

I obeyed his instruction as he walked around to the other end of the bed. I moved with his hands as he pulled me back so that my knees were on the edge of the mattress. Travis dropped to his knees, and I rested my toes on his shoulders for balance as he licked my inner thigh. I gasped as he moved to the other side, my throbbing pussy anticipating his touch.

Travis took his time, languidly moving his tongue along my thighs and to my lower lips. Sliding along them, he moved achingly slowly to reach my folds. One hand rested on the top of my ass, holding me still, while he stroked himself slowly with the other. I cried out as the tip of his tongue found my clit and swirled around it. He held me in place as I began to squirm while he teased and pressed into my sensitive pearl. I could feel the coming rush of an orgasm and closed my eyes, holding on to the comforter in tightly gripped fingers.

The tension rose until I couldn't take it anymore, and I screamed as he plunged his tongue inside me. The climax was heightened as his thumb moved to my clit while his tongue slid inside me, and I bucked against his grip. My toes curled, and I moaned as each rolling crash of climax took control.

Standing, Travis wasted no time in flipping me onto my stomach and positioning himself behind me. I rose up onto my knees and begged for him to enter me, crying out his name in desperation, the words melding together in the darkness and passion. I felt his head at my opening and braced myself. Then, with one mighty thrust, he was inside me, and my vision went white.

My voice escaped me, and my breath caught as the line between pain and pleasure was blurred. I pounded on the mattress and pressed my hips into him, inviting the pain, inviting the pressure as he filled me, stretched me. Strong, kneading fingers gripped my ass and hips, and he rocked back and then into me again. I cried out for more, and he increased his speed, leaving me dizzy and blinded by the sensation overwhelming my senses completely.

After a few moments, I found myself flipped over and his body crashing onto mine. One of his knees was on the bed, but the other still on the ground, giving him leverage to thrust deeply into me. Power to control me, to smother me with his body. My senses were filled with nothing but the heat of his breath, the tingling of my core and the sweat I licked from his chest.

The tension was building in me again, and his thrusts were frantic and labored. I clasped his face in both my hands, and our eyes locked as he came, exploding into me.

The feel of him filling me with his seed made me come too, and we rolled through the orgasm together, my body pulsing as he emptied inside me. Finally, he collapsed into my arms and kissed the beads of sweat from my neck, and I pulled a blanket over us to keep us warm.

CHAPTER 23

TRAVIS

I wasn't sold on that being the smartest decision of my life, but considering some of the really, really bad ones I had made, it certainly wasn't the worst either. And I didn't regret it. Not even for a second. As I lay there in her bed, a blanket draped over our naked bodies as we slowed our heartbeats and calmed down from the explosion of passion that had overtaken us, I smiled. A real, true, honest to God smile. For once, things seemed like they should be. Or at least close.

I didn't even regret it when Carrie rolled over and sat up, pulling her clothes up off the floor. I sat up too, taking the hint, and looked for my boxers. I knew they were some-where near my pants, but I couldn't find those either. Carrie stood, and I couldn't help but admire her as she bent over to pick up her panties off the floor and slip them back on. She turned to look at me and caught me staring, a grin stretching up one side of her mouth. She bent back down, and suddenly my boxers and jeans were airborne, flying toward me.

"I hate to do this," she said, "but Tina will be here with Amelia in a few minutes. I didn't realize what time it was."

"It's okay," I said. "No worries."

She offered a half-smile and grabbed her bra to put it back on. Then she crossed the room and opened a drawer and pulled out a pair of sweatpants.

Sighing silently, I put on my boxers and jeans and searched until I found my socks. Throwing them on, I looked around for my shirt but couldn't find it. Carrie saw me looking around confused and walked up to the lamp, where my shirt had found itself draped over the shade.

"Ah," I said, "there it is."

"Well, we were in a hurry to get it off," Carrie said. There was a note of flirtation there, but it was also kind of flat. Like the moment was over, and now she was far more concerned with me being there when Amelia got home than she was with any postcoital silliness.

I put the shirt back on and began the search for my shoes.

"I think I have everything," I said as I put the shoes back on.

"I'm sorry," she said again. "I just don't know how to explain this to a six-year-old yet, you know?"

"I promise, it's okay. I understand."

I wanted to kiss her. Mostly to prove that what had happened there wasn't some wild fit of fancy where we lacked reason and maturity but was instead something budding between us again. A spark that had been reignited.

But something held me back. She stood, waiting at the doorway to her room, one arm on the door and the other crossed over her stomach, holding on to the crook of the other arm. It was a pensive stance, and one that seemed almost annoyed. At any rate, I didn't think she would be terribly receptive to a kiss. So, I brushed by her and made my way to the front door. Opening it, I checked outside to see if Tina was back yet and then ducked my head back in.

"Coast is clear," I said. "I'll call you later?"

"Sounds good," she said. She hadn't moved from the bedroom door. I forced out a smile and waved.

"Bye," I said.

"Bye, Travis," she said, finally walking closer and taking the doorknob as I made my way out. She shut the door quietly behind me, and I walked to my car. As I got in, I looked up at her window to see if she was watching me leave like she used to when we were kids. She wasn't. I could barely make out her back as she walked into the kitchen and began to do something at the sink.

I drove home, and as soon as I was in the door, I plopped down on my couch. It was still early in the evening, but I was too tired to do much of anything, and too jacked up in the head to concentrate anyway. Briefly I thought about turning on one of the video games that sat neglected in the entire time I had been in Monroe due to the busy schedule and the sudden revelation that I was a father.

Before I could reach over and pick up a controller, I got a whiff of the smell coming off my skin. It was a combination of her scent and the unmistakable smell of sex. I dropped my head into my hands and sat in it for a moment, the emotions starting to bubble up. I had successfully avoided thinking about how awkward it all was all the way home, opting to play loud music and focus on the good aspects of the evening.

Now, all I could think about was the way she seemed distant and cold when I left. How she seemed uninterested in being with me, like I was a fling she'd picked up from a bar. It was messing with my brain. Maybe she was just feeling awkward about the situation and didn't know how to react. Maybe she was ashamed of falling into bed with me after everything that happened between us. Maybe she regretted it and would never make that mistake again.

No matter how she felt about it, I would respect her wishes. This much I knew. If that was as close to her as I would ever be again, I would have to accept that. It would be torture to be around her every time I saw Amelia. To know how that magic had reformed in an instant, how our bodies melded into one another like time had never passed. How gorgeous her body was under her clothes and how perfectly she still knew how to please me. How her body shook when she came.

It would all be so hard to forget and ignore, but I would have to. For right then, the best course of action for me would be to try to move on for the night. It would start with a shower. Getting up, I grabbed a water bottle and headed for the bathroom to take a long, punishingly hot soak.

When I got out, I looked at the clock and realized I still had most of the evening to go. Not feeling in the mood for video games or going out to eat, I picked up my phone and called the only person close by who I thought might want to spend time with me.

"Hello?" Hank said on the other end of the line.

"Hey, Hank. You doing anything tonight?"

Hank arrived about a half-hour later, and when I opened the door, he stuck a plastic bag into my hands. Curious, I looked inside and was surprised to find a bunch of wooden toys. They looked like the kind you found in antique stores or recreated in southern restaurants that have a shop attached with lots of kitschy things.

"What is this?" I asked.

"I carved them," Hank said proudly. My eyes opened wide in surprise. They were amazing looking.

"Really?" I asked.

"Yeah," he said, coming into the living room and sitting a twelve-pack of root beer on the couch. "I figured that you were about six years behind on toys to give to the little one. Might as well start with a few from old Uncle Hank."

His grin was genuine and hopeful, and I laughed. I laughed so hard that tears began forming at the edges of my eyes, and I wasn't entirely sure they were only there because of how adorable and silly it was. I was touched. We might have started off a bit shaky when I came back, but I was glad to have Hank in my life.

"Thank you, Hank," I said, finally. "She is going to love these, I'm sure. This is so damn thoughtful."

"No trouble," he said. "I've been carving wood most of my life. Used to do it with..." He trailed off. "Never mind."

"No, it's okay. You carved like this with Dad? I never saw him do it."

"Well, it was years ago," Hank said. "Back before you were around and when you were real little. He got the shakes awful bad when you were small, and it made it hard for him to carve anymore. He used to blame it on a problem with his nervous system, but you know."

I nodded. "I know."

"So, you said something about going to see her folks today," Hank said, referring to a phone call I'd had with him earlier. Ostensibly, I had called him to ask if he knew anything about her father and if there was something I could bring as an olive branch gift. His exact words were "other than that he's kind of a dick?"

"I did," I said, sitting down and opening the pack of root beer. It was a compromise. Hank still drank, but not to excess, and we both felt like having something special to drink when we had our chats. Hank suggested root beer as a joke, and I found that I loved the taste. I hadn't had it since I was little, probably at Hank's house, but the taste had a nostalgic feeling that I didn't get much since my past didn't have many good memories.

"Well, how'd it go?" he asked.

I told him about how her father almost immediately launched into me and how Carrie had stood up for me. I didn't extend that to the drive home or what happened after I got Carrie in her apartment, but he seemed to get that whatever was happening between me and her was a bit more complicated than a platonic parent situation. When I told him about how her father looked like he was ready for violence and then backed down, and almost seemed on the verge of being apologetic, Hank laughed.

"They might have been thinking they were doing the right thing back then, all those years ago," he said, taking a sip of the soda, "but really, like most of this town, they thought you were going to end up just like your old man."

I nodded. "Yeah."

"Now don't get me wrong," he said. "I loved your dad like a brother. He was my partner in silliness as a kid, and we grew up going to school and going to work and going to the bar together. I would have his back six days a week and twice on Sunday. But that man was a damn mess by the time you were little, and there's no use in denying it.

"You're just like your father, but in the good ways. You have his laugh and his sense of humor. But you are *nothing* like your father in the important ways. You ought to remember that."

CHAPTER 24

CARRIE

I was bursting at the seams to talk to Tina about what happened with Travis. When she came in with Amelia, I tried to detour her so I could snag even just a couple of minutes to tell her, but she was in a hurry.

"I'm so sorry I have to run. I have a million things to do," she said, heading for the front door.

"Already?" I asked, hoping my voice didn't come out quite as desperate as I thought it sounded, but at the same time kind of hoping it did because that might encourage her to stay.

"Yeah," she said. "I'm really sorry. I have a ton to do for work, and then I have errands." She let out an exasperated sound. "It's just a lot. I kind of let things build up, and now I'm paying for it. I'm sorry. I promise, though, I'll come hang out this week and we'll talk."

"Okay."

She stopped and looked at me. "Are you alright? Something seems different."

That could have been a moment when I just let it blurt

out, but I held it in. She didn't have time to talk, and this was definitely something we needed to talk about.

"I'm fine. Just let me know when you can come over," I said.

She nodded and gave me a hug before hurrying out. It took another two days for her to get everything done and be able to come over again. I ordered pizza and Amelia, Tina, and I sat around watching movies as we ate. As the evening grew later, it was time for my daughter to get ready for bed. She took her bath and got in her pajamas, then brought a book to Tina so she could read to her.

They hurried me out of the room, and I laughed as I went to clean up in the kitchen. There was still some pizza left in the box, so I brought it with me into the living room and dropped down onto the couch to wait for Tina.

It seemed Amelia was milking every bedtime story out of Tina she possibly could, and it was almost an hour before she came back into the living room. By that point, I thought I was going to lose my mind waiting. I needed to get the big secret out. If nothing more than just to say it out loud.

Besides, if Tina found out that something happened between Travis and me and I didn't tell her, she would flip.

Finally, Tina came back into the room and let out a dramatic sigh. "I'm telling you. That girl can listen to bedtime stories with the best of them. It's exhausting."

I wanted to laugh at her teasing, but as soon as my mouth opened, the secret fell out.

"I slept with Travis."

Tina gave me a questioning look as she flipped open the pizza box and reached in for another slice. The cheese stretched out a few inches, and she used her fingers to sever it before twirling it into a neat little pile on the top of the slice.

"I know," she said. "That's how you got Amelia."

She brought the slice to her mouth quickly to catch the cheese before it tumbled off. I stared at her for a few seconds, waiting for what I said to process all the way through her mind, but she just chewed and stared back at me. She clearly wasn't getting it.

"Yes, Tina. That is how I got Amelia. Thank you for the recap. But that's not what I meant," I said.

A tinge of red on her cheeks told me she was starting to come around.

"What?" she asked around another bite of pizza and used one finger to poke a slice of black olive back from where it tried to tumble out of the corner.

"I slept with Travis. That night we went over to talk to Mom and Dad. It wasn't like it was planned or anything. I got into an argument with Dad, and it was pretty intense. When Travis and I left, I was still worked up from it and it just kind of... happened," I said.

"It just kind of... happened?" Tina asked. "I better get more than that. Who started it? How did it start? Was it good? Oh, my gosh, I need it all." She took another bite, and her eyes widened. "Did one of you say that?"

I laughed and reached for my own piece of pizza. This was the conversation I was hoping for.

"I can't honestly say that specific phrase came out of either one of our mouths, but the sentiment was there. And I started it," I said.

She grinned. "That's my girl."

"I still can't even believe I did it. We were just driving back to my house, and I suddenly couldn't stop thinking about how good we were together and how much I wanted him. I tried to ignore it. I told myself I had to just ignore it and not do anything about it."

"Why?" Tina asked, sounding horrified I would even consider something like that.

"Because it would just make things more complicated. It's not like we're together or anything. We are barely even associating as friends. It's been all about Amelia. But it didn't do any good. As soon as we stopped, I kissed him. Part of me felt like maybe he would be the responsible one and stop me." I laughed.

"But he didn't," Tina said with a mischievous note in her voice.

"No, he didn't," I said, shaking my head and smiling.

I watched as Tina's face got redder and redder as I described the entire encounter. When I finished, she shook her head.

"O-M-G," she said.

I quirked an eyebrow at her. "Did you just say 'O-M-G'?"

She nodded. "I did. It was the only thing I could think of that seemed appropriate in this moment. I am seriously in disbelief right now."

"I know. Me, too. I keep wondering if maybe I just made it all up in my mind. I had some sort of sexy break from reality or something." I shook my head. "But no. It definitely happened."

"So, what now? What comes next?" Tina asked.

I let out a breath, some of the smile fading from my face. "I have no idea. The thing is, we still haven't talked about it. We haven't talked about anything. I haven't heard from him. So, I don't know what's going on."

"How do *you* feel about it?" she asked.

"I'm really conflicted. I never stopped loving him. You know that. Not really, anyway. It's always been in the back of my mind. But this whole situation is so tangled up. I don't know if I can give him an honest second chance," I said. "After all this time, I don't know if I can really bring myself to trust him again. We're such different people now. Maybe we wouldn't work anymore."

"Well, that's something you have to figure out, right?" Tina asked. "This happened and it happened for a reason. You just have to figure out what that reason is and what you want to do about it."

Tina was right. My encounter with Travis had changed everything. The situation was completely different now, and I had to really think about it and figure out what it all meant. I had to decide what to do next because it wasn't fair for any of us to drag it out if it wasn't going to end up with us as a solid family.

From the beginning, my big worry about bringing Travis into our lives was him leaving again and hurting Amelia. I knew what it was like to have him just disappear, and I couldn't bear the thought of her going through something even close to that. Making the decision to let him get to know her and form a relationship with her was a risk. Now that risk was even higher.

There was no room for ambiguity or uncertainty between us. Not with Amelia in our lives. I had to know for sure that we were going to end up as the family she deserved, or completely step back and just let them have their relationship separate from everything else. It was the only way to protect her and stop this situation from getting even messier and more difficult than it already was.

The problem was, I didn't know what to do or how to figure it out.

CHAPTER 25

TRAVIS

It had been several days since Carrie and I ended up in bed together, and it was on my mind pretty much constantly. It didn't help that we hadn't talked about it yet. It followed me everywhere—at work, at the gym that I recently joined, at home. Everywhere I went, my mind went into default mode thinking about Carrie and how what happened between us might have endangered any growth that was happening. It bugged me that we hadn't talked about it, or talked at all, since then. One thing I knew for sure was that I didn't want to call her and seem needy or pushy. She was obviously not contacting me for a reason. I just wished I knew why.

As much as I put my head down to focus and tried to get through it all without it affecting me, it did anyway. Those thoughts and questions would creep in anytime I had downtime. If I sat down for more than thirty seconds, my mind would drift to the way her body felt in my hands, and then the way she looked when I left. And the fact that we hadn't said anything since then. I tried to push it out of my mind every time, and it would go, but not for long. As soon as I was sitting down or had a moment for my mind to wander, the questions were back again.

It was the day before Valentine's Day, and thankfully things were pretty slow. I was glad to have a few days where things were relatively calm. Regular patients came and went, and a few slips and falls or mysterious rashes brought some kids in, but otherwise, I ended up helping out in the ER for large portions of time.

Things had gotten so slow that Dr. Jones sent me out on a gopher mission, asking me to pick up some mint tea. He was apparently fond of it in the winter, and there was none in the hospital.

When I came back, I dropped the tea off in the break-room and went to the refrigerator. It was dangerous, but Hank had spawned a sudden and intense obsession with root beer, and I was up to a can a day. Considering that my day was almost over, and things were slow enough that I might be sent out early, I figured now was as good a time as any to have my daily soda. Dr. Jones came in and saw me, then the tea sitting next to the sink, and then looked back to me.

"Did you get the message?" he asked.

"What message?"

"You had a message over the intercom. It must have been right before you got in the building. Someone is waiting for you in the ER. Not a patient," he said.

"Oh?" I asked, hope rising in my voice. Dr. Jones seemed to catch on.

"An older gentleman," he said in that patient and yet cautious way a person says things that they hope doesn't cross any lines that they weren't aware of. When my face turned down, he seemed to nod, not in agreement of my life choices but more in general acknowledgement of knowing which way the wind blew.

"Well, I guess I better go see who it is," I said, standing.

"What time was your shift ending?" Dr. Jones asked.

"Eight," I said. He pulled up his smartwatch and looked at it for a moment.

"Seven thirty now," he said. "Why don't you go ahead and clock out."

"Sure," I said. "See you tomorrow."

"Ah yes, Valentine's Day," he said with a cocked eyebrow.

I smiled, not wanting to tell him I didn't really have anyone to spend the holiday with.

"Thanks, Dr. Jones," I said.

"Very welcome. Now get out of here," he said.

I followed his advice and clocked out, heading to the ER to see who was waiting for me. I was absolutely dumbfounded by who I found. Carrie's dad sat in one of the plush chairs overlooking the road, a coffee from our complimentary maker in his hand. He sipped it absentmindedly before noticing I was in the room and standing.

"Mr. Jacobs," I said in acknowledgement.

"Travis," he said. "I came to ask you a question." He looked like he would rather be literally anywhere else in the world than standing in front of me at the hospital. It was the look of a little kid being made to apologize for something he didn't think was wrong.

"Sure," I said. "What's on your mind?"

"Well, I came to extend an invitation to dinner tomorrow. No pressure."

I noticed how quickly he added the no pressure portion

of his message. As if urging me to say no and giving me an out to do so. Still, I was dumbfounded.

"Are you sure?" I asked.

He shuffled where he stood, looking at the ground as if it was suddenly the most interesting tile he had ever seen before.

"Yes," he said. "We've been doing a Valentine's feast for Amelia since she was very little, and it's become a bit of a tradition. Both Carrie and the missus think it would be a good idea for you to be there for Amelia."

He wasn't happy about it. He made that expressly clear. That said, it was a huge deal to be invited, and knowing Mr. Jacobs as I did, I didn't want to take any chances. I held out my hand, which he looked at curiously for a moment before shaking.

"I'd love that," I said. "I have to be here for a bit tomorrow, but I can come over right after that. What time?"

"You can coordinate with Carrie about that," he said. "I'll see you there."

Releasing my hand, Mr. Jacobs promptly walked to the door and left, leaving me standing there in the middle of the ER waiting room. I had a surprised smile on my face, and I shook my head to try to clear the cobwebs. Pulling out my phone, I hit the contact for Carrie, and she picked up on the second ring.

"Hey," she said. There was excitement in her voice, even if there was a note of apprehension. The part of me that was sure I needed to let her contact me was suddenly questioning its judgment.

"Hi, Carrie," I said. "Guess who I just spoke to?"

"I have no idea," she said without waiting for the question to gain any more time.

"Your father."

"Oh no."

"No, he didn't come to argue," I said.

"Really?" Carrie asked. "Then what was he there for?"

"To invite me to dinner with you guys tomorrow."

"Wait, what?" Carrie said again, and I laughed at the inflection of her voice.

"Yeah," I said. "I told him yes, so be prepared for that. Also, I have no idea what time I'll be able to come by. I do have to be here at the hospital tomorrow. Should I just head over after that?"

"Yes," Carrie said. She still seemed shocked by what I told her. To be fair, I was shocked too. "I think this is a good thing," she said finally.

"You do?" I asked. "I'm not walking into a trap or anything? No shotguns waiting on the other end of the door, or anything like that?"

"I don't think so," Carrie said, not seeming to notice the humor part of the joke.

"Filling me with confidence there, Carrie."

"Sorry," she said. "I just think that you coming over and doing Valentine's dinner with us should work wonders for fixing some of the past. It's kind of a tradition we started with her a few years ago. We make everything red and pink and there's lots of sweets and she loves it. Being there with Amelia over a holiday will also go a long, long way."

"I agree," I said, heading to the outside and the cold of the bitter winter. "But if we are going to do this, we need to do it right. Which means I have something I have to go do. Remind me again, what's your mother's favorite color?"

"Purple," she said. "What are you going to do?"

"It's a surprise I'll call you when I'm on my way over tomorrow," I said.

"Alright." There was silence for a moment, and then in

a voice that warmed my heart considerably, she said, "I look forward to it. I'm excited."

"Good. I am too."

I hung up the phone feeling more hopeful than I had in years.

CHAPTER 26

CARRIE

I helped my mother plate the pasta with red sauce, the ham with candied apples, and the homemade dinner rolls to which my mother always added a drop of pink food coloring just for Amelia.

We set everything on the table and I began pouring Amelia a cup full of pink lemonade when there was a knock at the door. I hurried to beat my father to it and my eyes widened when I opened the door only to see three humongous bouquets of roses with legs and feet.

Travis dropped them down a bit so they weren't covering his face and grinned. My heart jumped in my chest and my palms began to sweat as I took in the man that I knew I'd never stop loving.

Amelia rushed up beside me and grinned up at Travis. "Hi Daddy! Are those for me?" she asked.

Travis knelt down and handed our daughter a bouquet of baby pink roses. "Happy Valentine's Day sweetheart," he said with a smile that matched hers.

Amelia marveled over the flowers for a moment before

whirling around and bounding off to the kitchen to show her grandmother.

"I think you just made her whole day," I told him, stepping aside so he could enter the house.

He came inside and held out a beautiful bouquet of deep red roses to me and bent to place a quick peck on my cheek.

I looked up at him and smiled, my insides tingling and warm as I lifted the roses to my nose and breathed deeply.

My mother walked into the hall just then and Travis held out the last bouquet toward her. The dark purple roses were exquisite, and she couldn't help but smile widely at them as she took them from his hands.

"Happy Valentine's Day Mrs. Jacobs. Thank you for inviting me to dinner with you tonight."

My mother nodded her head at Travis. "You are most welcome. And thank you for the flowers. They are breathtaking." She turned to go back to the kitchen to put them in water and I raised an eyebrow at him.

"Sucking up to my mother?" I asked him.

He shrugged and grinned again. "Hey, whatever works."

I ushered Travis into the dining room where Amelia demanded he sit next to her. Dinner was lovely and went off without a hitch. Afterward, we had slices of a rich red velvet cake with pink cream cheese frosting that I had made earlier that day. We sat in the living room in front of the fire for a while and managed pleasant conversation. Overall, I was very pleased with how things turned out.

It was getting late and Amelia needed to get to bed so we bundled her up and got her into the car.

"Would you mind if I followed you home?" Travis asked.

I looked up at him quizzically. What was he thinking?

Before I could ask, he said, "I'd really like to tuck my daughter in tonight if that's okay."

I couldn't help but smile, that rush of warmth returning to cascade through my body. "Sure. I think she would really like that.

When we got to my place, Travis got out of his car and came to my window.

"I'll carry her inside," he said.

I nodded, and he gathered her up again. I gathered up the bouquets of flowers and the boxes of chocolates that Travis had left in his car just for Amelia and me.

As Travis was in with Amelia, I went into the kitchen to make a pot of tea. Travis came out of Amelia's bedroom with a smile on his face.

"She woke up just enough to ask me to read to her," he said. "I don't think she was even still awake by the time I started reading. But I read three books just to make sure."

I laughed. "That's pretty good coverage. Can I make you a cup of tea?"

He nodded. "That sounds good."

When the tea was ready, we brought it into the living room, and both of us let out heavy breaths when we sank into the couch.

For a few minutes, we sipped our tea and watched the light snow falling outside the window. Then I looked at him and realized just how good he looked sitting there in the house. I set down my cup and leaned over to kiss him.

I meant to just kiss him and see where it went, but the second our lips touched, I knew I wanted more. There was no denying he did too by the bulge in his pants that strained against the zipper. I broke the kiss to look into his eyes and realized there was no use denying myself. I wanted him.

The house was quiet, and Amelia was in her room with the door shut. Where we were on the couch, I would hear her door open and have time to get ourselves in order.

I climbed on top of him, straddling him, and the growl that rolled through his chest made me weak in the knees. I sat down onto his lap and felt that bulge pushing up into my core and rocked my hips on him. We kissed again, our tongues tangling with one another, and I reveled in the taste of him. If this was a bad idea, it was the best kind of bad idea.

Travis's hands gripped my ass and squeezed as he guided me through my rocking motion. Very slowly, I leaned back, leaving his lips pursed from our kiss. He opened his eyes to watch as I unbuttoned the top button of my blouse. I bit my bottom lip as I continued down the front, unbuttoning each one with a little bit of dramatic flair. I wanted him to want me as much as I wanted him, to make him nearly beg me for it.

When the last button was undone, I slid it off my shoulders, letting it fall inch by inch until it pooled at my wrists and around the back of my waist. I rocked again on him and pressed my breasts into his face. His tongue slid out to lick between them, and I pulled the sleeves off and let the blouse fall to the floor. As he ran his tongue across my chest, I reached behind me and undid the bra, which released my heavy breasts.

He groaned below me and reached up to knead them. Drawing his tongue across, he filled his mouth with my nipple and sucked while I rocked on him harder. I let my head fall back and my eyes close as I focused on the sensation of his soft, strong tongue on my body. My breath hitched, and I groaned softly as his hands squeezed and kneaded me.

I stood, pulling his lips from my breasts, my bare feet on the cushions of the couch. Unbuttoning my pants, I swayed my hips as I pulled them down to my knees. At that point, he reached up to help me remove them from my legs, and I kicked them away when they were gone. I continued rocking my hips toward him, bringing my core closer and closer to his mouth. His hot breath on my sensitive skin only drove me more intensely mad. Finally, his lips were brushing the soft pink fabric of my panties.

Reaching down, I pulled the fabric to the side, and he licked me from the entrance to the top. I gasped, and he reached up to pull the panties down and off me. I placed one knee on the backrest of the couch, and he dove his face into my core, his talented and familiar tongue sliding through my folds. He found my clit and began to tease it. I grabbed at him, pulling him closer by cradling him on the back of his neck. A finger slid inside me, and I nearly screamed, slamming my hand over my mouth to muffle the sound.

It didn't take long before my hips rocked again, his tongue flickering over my clit and his finger brushing the top wall of my pussy in rapid motions. I felt the climax coming and didn't wait to let it take control. I crushed his head into me and held him there as I came, my breath hitching and my eyes lolling back. I shook violently as the orgasm took over my body, and when I finally felt in control again, I slid back down him to his lap.

My body was buzzing, but he was unfairly clothed. I placed my lips on his as I scooted off his lap and then draped my top half over it. Travis slid his hand between my thighs and continued to touch me as I desperately pulled at his zipper. He shifted his hips so I could pull the pants down enough to get a grasp on the base of his cock and pull it through. Immediately, I took him into my mouth, and the rumbling groan in his chest vibrated down and onto my tongue.

I could feel him unbuttoning his shirt and pants as I bobbed up and down on him, taking him deeply into my throat. His cock stiffened to the point that it strained in my lips, and I grasped the base to stroke him as I sucked him. He moaned and placed one hand on the back of my head to guide me to take him deeper while the other hand grabbed my breast. Pulling him out of my mouth with a little pop of suction brought another moan from deep inside his chest, and I locked eyes with him. He motioned to me, and I knew what he meant. I always did.

Climbing back on top of him, I positioned my pussy just above the tip of his massive cock. I held it by the base and brushed the head through my folds, sending shock waves of pleasure through my tingling body. Then, straddling him, I placed him at the entrance and slowly sat down. He filled me completely, and I had to take my time going down, occasionally rising a little before sinking further, so my body could adjust to him.

Finally, I was sitting fully on his lap, his throbbing, hard cock deep inside me. It was like he was made just for my body. I rocked on him, and it brought parts of me alive that I thought had long been dead before our first tumble into bed. I locked my lips to his, and he guided my hips in slow but increasingly faster motions. Soon, I was riding him hard, my hands gripping the back of the sofa, and his lips clasped over my breast.

Another orgasm washed over me as I slammed down onto him, taking him into me fully, and I held myself there. As my body pulsed, he picked me up and slowly laid me on the floor. His hips didn't stop pounding into me, and when I was on my back, he reached up to clasp my hands. Raising them above my head, he held them tightly as his body curled over mine. I wrapped my legs around him, crossing my ankles above his ass as he continued to thrust deeper, harder and faster into my pussy.

Travis's ear was just beside my lips as he grunted with effort, and I sucked on the lobe. His labored breath brushed my neck, and I felt my skin react and my hair rise at the sensation. His cock continued to pound into me, and I could feel him edging closer and closer to a finishing point. My core was throbbing with him, and my vision started to fill with spots as I relaxed into his control.

His large, muscular body rubbed against mine with each thrust, my breasts sliding against rock-hard pecs. Suddenly, he sat up and I instinctively raised my legs. It was a position I remembered well. Draping my legs over his shoulders, he bent me in half and our eyes locked. The intensity in them as he pumped into me drove my arousal higher, and I felt the unbelievable wave of yet another climax about to take control. The tension built insanely fast, and I moaned in short, yipping sounds as I clamped my hand over my mouth.

Sweat beaded on his skin and fell onto my lips as I held my mouth open, unable to make any more sound. I raised my head, and our lips crushed into one another as the wave began to crash around me. Suddenly he pulled away from the kiss and strained his upper body, his muscles bulging as he slammed into me as hard as he could. His jaw opened, and his eyes clenched shut. My world went dizzy and white.

We came together. His cock exploded into me and filled me as I throbbed and milked him. Each intense pulse brought more pleasure, and I clawed at the carpet for control. Finally, he emptied himself fully and collapsed into my arms. I kissed the top of his head and down his cheek until I reached his lips. We stayed that way for a little while before retiring to bed, where we started again an hour later and fell asleep exhausted and satisfied.

CHAPTER 27

TRAVIS

Twice had to mean something, right? People didn't just fall into bed with the same person more than once and have it not mean that something was there. Something was there that we both obviously wanted and wanted to pursue. Right?

Confusion was banging down the door of my mental state, but I tried to refuse it entry. I was too busy being warm and comfortable in her bed. Apparently, Amelia had a habit of sometimes sleepwalking into her mother's bed, so we put clothes back on. Thankfully, I always kept a spare set of clothes in the car in case I needed a shower or to hazmat the clothes I was wearing. They were a simple white T-shirt and a pair of scrubs pants, but they were good enough for sleeping in. I brought them in quietly while Carrie went to the bathroom and put them on before slipping beneath her covers.

They came off again like an hour later when we found ourselves entangled again, but then I slipped them back on and curled up next to her to sleep.

I drifted in and out of sleep all night, but it wasn't

fitful. I just kept waking up and opening my eyes, making sure it was real. I was really in her bed, I was really holding her, and the sun was really rising. No matter how many times I woke up, I still believed in that second before I opened my eyes that it would have all been a dream. But it never was, and I would grin and fall back to sleep.

She shifted in her sleep once and rolled over to curl into my chest, and it woke me up long enough to smile. That same smile was on my face when I woke up again a bit later, but Carrie wasn't there. A brief second of panic went through me before I realized I was in her bedroom, wearing the scrubs pants and still smelling like her. I relaxed into the mattress and let my mind wake up a little more before sitting up and putting my socks back on.

Voices carried down the hall, and when I made it out of the bedroom, I could tell they were coming from the kitchen. The smell of bacon was filling up the house, and my stomach rumbled. Still a little groggy, I entered the kitchen and embraced Carrie from behind, pressing a kiss to her cheek. It was just like old times when her parents would go away for the weekend or we would go off on a getaway pretending she was with Tina and stay in a hotel.

Except for the squealing voice of a six-year-old, who woke me fully from my grogginess, and was punctuated by a zombie-like stare from Carrie as she whipped around to face me. She was clearly not quite fully awake and unprepared for whatever was about to happen. In that moment, I knew we had to talk. Not knowing where we stood, especially after last night, was going to make me start spiraling, and I most certainly didn't need that.

Amelia hopped out of her chair at the kitchen table and pounced on my leg. I picked her up and carried her into the living room as she babbled excitedly at me. She wrapped her arms around my neck as she talked.

"I asked Santa to bring me my daddy. He was a little late, but you still got here," she said.

I felt a twist in my heart when she said those words and then threw herself around my neck to hug me again. "Yep, I got here baby. And I'm going to be here forever."

"Come eat breakfast," Carrie said from the kitchen. Amelia's eyes went wide.

"I forgot. I was so excited to see Daddy. Sorry, Mommy!" she said as I brought her back in. I sat her at her chair and then waited for Carrie to sit down. Carrie sat a plate in front of me and took her seat beside Amelia.

We ate without addressing each other, content to let Amelia fill the silence with more talk about all the Valentines she got from all of her classmates. I had also given her the toys Hank had made for her and she gushed about how much she loved them, which I knew was going to delight him to no end.

I figured Carrie would tell Amelia to go play, but every time it seemed like she was about to, the little girl would take one of our hands and ask us to help her put together a new toy or to play with her. Finally, Amelia asked to go play with her new toys in her room, and Carrie agreed. When she was gone, Carrie walked silently back into the kitchen and poured some coffee before coming back in and sitting down across from me on the couch where our night had really begun. I noticed, out of the corner of my eye, that she had forgotten her panties in her clothes gathering last night. They were tucked under the couch leg. I was going to address them when Carrie cleared her throat and checked to make sure Amelia wasn't in the room.

"You can't do this to me," she whispered.

"Excuse me?" I said, keeping my voice low.

"This," she said. "Amelia. You can't just tell her you're going to stick around forever like we're a real family and build her hopes up like that. It could crush her."

"What?"

"You just let her believe we were together and that you'd be staying forever. That's unfair of you," she said.

"Hang on a minute." Anger began to rise in my chest. "*You* are the one who had me stay last night. At any point you could have raised an objection and told me to go home."

"Yeah, that would have gone over well I'm sure," she said, settling back into the couch and sipping her coffee. It was like she was regretting last night again, and I couldn't take it. This roller coaster had to stop.

"Look, I don't want to tell her that we aren't a family," I said.

"Figures," she interrupted.

"Because it's what I want too," I said.

Slowly, she lowered the cup from her lips, and her eyes burned into mine. Then, they grew softer, and I knew something had just changed. I wasn't sure what yet, or if it was good or not, but the tone of the conversation was different. The anger faded away. I scooted to the edge of the chair I was in to get closer to her as her brows furrowed in what looked like confusion.

"I don't want to tell her we aren't a family because I believe that is exactly what we are supposed to be," I said. "I know I wasn't here when she came, and I've been absent all this time. But I am here now, and I'm ready, and I think you are too. But you need to decide what you want, because we can't string her or each other along anymore. I've never stopped loving you. Never. But I need you to make a decision, Carrie. Hopefully sooner rather than later."

With that, I stood. I made my way back down the hall to the bedroom and gathered my clothes that I had put into a pile together by the bed. Balling them up, I stuck them under my arm and brought them to the living room where I grabbed my empty duffel and stuffed them inside.

Carrie was still on the couch, the coffee still in her hands as she stared into the middle distance. I didn't know where she was going to end up, but I knew where I wanted her to. I had laid it all out on the line for her, and she just needed to choose if it was worth it to her to have a relationship with me the way that I clearly wanted with her and that Amelia was pining for.

I didn't want to pressure her or guilt-trip her, though. It had to be her decision and hers alone. She needed to want to be with me, the way we were, but also in a newer, more adult way. A way that wouldn't be broken apart by the opinions of her father and mother or anyone else on the planet.

Making my way back down the hall, I ducked into Amelia's room, and she saw me over the playhouse she was fiddling with. Tossing down her Barbie dolls, she ran to me and wrapped me in a hug again. I smiled at her little arms around my neck, and a twinge of loss clenched my heart at all the hugs I had missed out on in the first years of her life.

"Okay kiddo,I have to go to work," I said. It was a lie, and I felt bad about it, but I had to say something to get out of the house. I couldn't be there in Carrie's presence at that moment. "But I will see you very soon."

"Will you come home after you get off?" she asked. Worry seemed to cross her little face, but I smiled, and it immediately lessened.

"I'm not sure," I said. "I work really late tonight, and it might be better if I go back to my place near the hospital. You probably would be asleep before I got off anyway."

"But I like you here with us," she said, falling back into my arms for another hug. I patted her back and sighed.

"I know. But not tonight, okay? We have big plans for Saturday, though, right?" I asked. Her little eyes lit up at the reminder of our planned outing to the local ice skating rink. When I had suggested it a few days ago, Amelia was beside herself with excitement.

"Will I get to hold both you and Mama's hand when I skate?" she asked. I smiled.

"Of course you will," I said. "Now be a good girl for your mama and I'll see you later, okay?"

"Okay, Daddy," she said, hugging me again before turning back to her toys and diving down behind the playhouse and into her own world again.

I walked back into the living room one last time, but Carrie had left. She was in the kitchen, doing dishes. Part of me wanted to go in there and help, maybe be able to parlay that into another discussion about where she was. But I couldn't. I already told Amelia I was leaving, and if I pushed Carrie, it might turn into an argument which wasn't what I wanted.

It was better to just walk out the door. Grabbing my coat and slipping it on, that's just what I did. When I got outside into the bitter cold, I pulled my coat tight over me and got into the car, turning the engine and getting the heat going despite the short drive. As I backed out, I could see in the window a tiny face and a tiny hand waving me goodbye. I waved back, and just before I drove away, I saw Carrie's face at the window beside her. She didn't wave, and I couldn't read the expression on her face.

CHAPTER 28

CARRIE

I couldn't believe I'd just done that. It was like it wasn't even me. Like I was hearing somebody else use my voice to push back against Travis. My reaction didn't make any sense, and yet when I opened my mouth, it was the only thing that came out.

I couldn't blame Travis for his response, but my heart was a mess as I watched him go. This whole situation was so confusing, so tangled up and difficult to dig my way through. It was hard enough when I was just trying to grapple with my own feelings for Travis and figure out what they might mean after our first night together.

Now things had taken another turn and were only more complicated. We couldn't keep our hands off each other. I couldn't resist him, even when I tried to. Ending up in bed together again made things exponentially more challenging, but Amelia really pushed it over the edge.

She wasn't supposed to see any of it. I didn't want her to see any type of relationship forming between Travis and me other than a friendship. Until we had made a real decision about what was going to happen between us and figured out what that would look like moving forward, I didn't want Amelia factoring into it. I didn't want her to see it and start coming up with her own conclusions.

Having Travis around in her mind needed to stay just about her. She needed to be able to continue to get to know him and form a bond with him without thinking about how we might feel for each other.

But now that was completely blown out of the water.

She immediately started thinking we were going to be together and that the three of us were going to be a happy family. And the thing was, Travis didn't argue it. In fact, he seemed all about it. He said that was what he wanted, he said that he'd never stopped loving me, and I wanted so much to believe him.

Everything in me wanted to believe what Travis said. I wanted to be able to just give in to it and finally let our little family enjoy being together. For so long, it had just been the two of us, and I had wondered what it would be like if Travis had never left and we'd stayed together. Or even if he had come home earlier in Amelia's life and we reconnected.

But I couldn't get rid of the voice in the back of my mind. I couldn't separate myself completely from the negative thoughts that swelled in my brain when I first found out Travis was back in town for three years. The pain of him leaving the way he did was still fresh in my mind. I was still filled with the anger and hurt that came from not only him leaving, but also him never trying to get in touch or come back to find me.

My first thought when I saw him at the bakery and started wondering about telling him about Amelia was that he wouldn't want anything to do with her. He wouldn't want to find out he was an instant father and start doing all the things fathers did.

In my mind, he couldn't even muster the decency to break up with me properly and had been away from town for seven years. There was no way he would find out he had a daughter he never even knew existed and get completely panicked about all the responsibilities he would have. He had taken so well to fatherhood, and both of them seemed to really be enjoying their time together.

But I didn't know if I could totally trust him. It made me feel horrible to even think that way, but there was a time when I thought our relationship was perfect and he made me so happy, and he ran off into the sunset anyway. There was no way of saying he wouldn't do it again. He might initially be excited about having a child, but then get over-whelmed and have to distance himself from it all. Being a parent wasn't always rainbows and roses. Some days it was really damn hard.

Even though Travis hadn't done anything to tell me that was the way he was going to be down the line, and had actu-ally shown me the total opposite, I was still very worried. Especially since it wasn't just about me anymore. It would be brutal for him to suddenly decide he didn't want anything to do with me anymore and cut me off, but it was worse now that Amelia was involved.

I called Tina, and she said she would be right over. Amelia had spread all her new toys out across the living room and was engrossed in a detailed make-believe game when she arrived. She lifted a paper bag that was exuding the most delicious smells and I knew she had grabbed carryout from my favorite Mexican restaurant in town.

We fixed our plates and ate while watching one of Amelia's favorite cartoons. After we were done, my daughter went right back into what she had been doing before Tina had shown up with lunch.

"Okay, spill," Tina said when we got to the kitchen and started washing the dishes. "What's going on?"

I let out a sigh. "I had sex with Travis again."

"Why does that strike me as something you shouldn't look so upset about?" she asked.

"It wouldn't be, maybe, if we'd talked about what was going on with us first. But we never got around to it. Everything has been busy, and then my parents invited him over. It was a lot. I meant to talk to him when we got back here. But then I looked over at him and he looked so good. Like he belonged here. So, I kissed him. I meant it to be only a kiss."

"It seems you've been having a lot of situations where you intend something to be just a kiss and it doesn't turn out that way lately."

"Yeah," I said with a sigh. "And it turned out just the way it did the last time. Only, this time he spent the night. I can't even believe I let that happen. But somewhere along the lines, we just got up, got ready for bed, and curled back up together."

"That's sweet," Tina said.

"Then Amelia the next morning—she was so excited and happy. She was talking about how she had asked Santa to bring her a daddy and even though he was late, she still got her wish. Then he told her he wasn't going anywhere ever again. And instead of just letting it happen, I shut it down. Then Travis asked what was going on and what I wanted, and I didn't even know what to say."

"Why?" Tina asked.

"I don't know. It was everything I ever wanted, but I couldn't bring myself to accept it. I don't even know how I'm supposed to feel. I still love him. I always have. But I have such a hard time trusting him. I can't bear the thought of him just leaving again. It would destroy Amelia if she got wrapped up in the idea of us being a family and then it didn't work out," I said.

"I hate to break this to you, Carrie, but that girl is already stuck like glue to her daddy. That's not something that would show up because he stayed around. It's already here. And besides, it's clear you want him. Why are you fighting yourself? Why can't this just be easy? Yes, things are different now, but that doesn't mean they have to be difficult. Just let it be what it is. He's back. Now focus on fixing what got fucked up and be the family you're supposed to be."

My best friend was right. I was fighting too hard against it when everything was right there in front of me. Now I knew it was my turn to go to him. He wasn't going to come back after the way I'd acted that morning. And he shouldn't. I needed to be the one to try this time.

"Will you watch Amelia?" I asked.

Tina nodded. "Of course."

"Thank you."

I ran to get dressed as fast as I could and rushed out to my car to head to Travis's house.

CHAPTER 29

TRAVIS

I got home and tossed my coat onto the couch. My mind was a mess, and the only thing I could think of doing was to work out. Working out usually helped focus my mind and get me into a better place. I dropped to the ground and began rattling off push-ups until my biceps were sore and screaming for a break. Then I hopped up and began doing squats until my calves burned. Then burpees until I was sweating and out of breath and collapsed.

After a few moments of delirium, where the questions about Carrie and Amelia finally broke away for a precious few seconds to let me focus on just being tired, I almost fell asleep. Suddenly, it all came back, and I slammed my hand on the floor and sat up. I contemplated doing roughly a billion crunches, but I knew it wouldn't help. Nothing was helping. So, instead, I got up and took a shower. I spent a long time under the hot water, letting it beat down on newly sore muscles and the neck that always tightened under stress.

But I felt no better clean than I had sweating. I had no plans on staying there in the tiny apartment, but I didn't know where to go either. I just needed to think for a little while. Pacing helped get out some of the renewed energy, and what started as angry speed-walking steps turned into slower, more contemplative ones as my body started to wear out. The entire situation played out in my head, and I was trying to get a grip on what it all meant and what I was supposed to do from here. Some of it just didn't make sense.

Stopping for a moment to get a glass of water, I went back to pacing, occasionally talking to myself out loud. I knew I was just steps from spiraling, and if it got much worse, I was going to have to do something else to keep myself from drinking. Calling my sponsor might not be enough. I might have to walk down to the hospital and clock myself in. Dr. Jones had offered that if I felt like it, I could pick up a few more hours at any time as long as it didn't affect my work with him on my regular schedule. Maybe work would give me the focus I needed to not be so out of my mind.

But I knew I was in no frame of mind to be treating patients. I was too wound up. Too confused. Too distracted. I tried putting myself in her shoes and working through it, and it still didn't seem right. We had been doing good. At least I thought we had been doing good, considering she kept kissing me. She kept getting close to me, and we spent more and more time together with Amelia. She even initiated both times we had fallen into bed together, and she had been stone-cold sober both times too. She didn't have an excuse.

Even her parents appeared to be coming around. Sure, it was going to be a long time before we were chummy or anything, but her dad had stopped finding little ways to insult me, and her mother was practically acting like I was just part of the family already. For the most part, this hurdle was jumped.

So, what else was it she wanted? Was she just working out some things from how I left, but she wasn't actually interested in me anymore? Was she just trying to keep me close so I would be there for our daughter? Was she falling as hard as I was and was just too afraid to admit it?

I had no answers, and it bugged the shit out of me. I was so tired of feeling like I had no control in the situation. So tired of feeling like I just had to wait around for other people to make decisions about how my life was going to be.

Suddenly, I stopped. I looked around the small, mostly empty apartment. It was too small for a family. And that's what I had now. A family.

I made a decision in that moment. One that I knew was going to change everything. I needed to be the one to fight. I couldn't walk away again, and I couldn't just wait on an answer. Carrie deserved me showing her that I was willing to fight for her. If that meant going and banging on her door and forcing her to have a hard conversation, that's exactly what I was going to have to do.

Grabbing my jacket in my hand, I turned to the door and yanked it open, the plan to run to Carrie's place and demand she talk in the center of my mind. I was in such a rush out the door that I nearly tripped over Carrie herself, who was standing there, her face a mask of wretched emotion. I stumbled and stopped, holding myself up in the doorway.

"I'm sorry," she said, before I could get my stunned lips or shocked vocal cords to force any words of surprise out.

"What?"

"Travis." Her hands twisted as she anxiously searched

for words. "Travis, you have to know... I never stopped loving you..."

It was all I needed to hear. I pounced on her, pulling her in for a deep, tearful kiss. She nearly sobbed on my shoulder for a moment before looking me in the eyes, a smile crossing her face.

"I love you," she said again, and our lips met once more. This time, I picked her up, my arms around her waist to pull her inside, out of the cold. "Where are we going?" she asked before we got inside.

"Is Amelia here?" I asked, suddenly worried she was in the car, waiting.

"No, Tina is watching her at home."

"Good." Bending down, I swept her legs up in my other arm and carried her over the threshold and into my living room. I didn't stop there, and she looked around a little before giggling and returning her lips to mine as I made our way to the bedroom and brought her to my bed.

We needed to talk, but after hearing her say she loved me, I needed to answer that.

"I love you too," I said. "I never stopped."

I collapsed into her arms on the bed, and we kissed for what seemed like an exquisite eternity, languidly relishing in the touch of our lips together. Slowly, I crawled between her legs and sat up. The heat in the room had kicked on a while ago, but the heat between us was enough to keep me warm with far less clothing. I pulled the shirt off, and her hands rose to run across my body.

Carrie's fingers trailed down my stomach to my sweatpants and pulled them down easily. My cock was stiff and sprung out at her. The devilish grin that crossed her face when it did made me smile, and as she grasped it by the base, she pulled at me so that I would straddle her chest.

She slid out her tongue and swirled it around the head, making me groan. She always knew just how to please me. Her full, luxurious lips wrapped around my cock, and her warm, wet mouth made it slick. I loved watching her bob back and forth on me as she stroked me into her. Her eyes sparkled when they opened, and we maintained eye contact as she sucked my cock.

I reached down and undid the button for her pants. Reaching down between my legs to her own, she pulled them off her in one quick yank and tossed them off the bed. I moved so that I was no longer straddling her and lay down on the bed facing the opposite way and wrapped her waist in my arm. Lifting her like she was weightless, I settled her over me on my back. I swept my tongue along her thighs as she dove back down on my cock with her mouth.

Licking her until her toes curled and she gasped as she stroked me, her face settling on my leg, I waited for the familiar buck of her hips. When she came, her body squirmed, and I held her tight with both arms, pressing my tongue deep inside her while she stuffed my staff in her mouth until the head brushed the back of her throat.

When her body stopped convulsing, she got off me, and I sat up. I wanted her to know how much I wanted her. How much I needed her. She let out a surprised yelp as I picked her up. Wrapping her legs around me, I put one hand under her ass to help her position herself. The other guided my cock to her opening. Our eyes were locked on one another as I slid inside her.

She was slick and hot, and her pussy pulsed as I penetrated deep inside. She cried out in pleasure as I lifted her up and down on me, then turned and pressed her back against the wall. Using it for leverage, I held her up with both hands under her and pounded into her. Her jaw was locked in an open position, but barely sound came out as I fucked her against the wall. My arms strained, but not because of weight, but out of resistance. I was holding myself back from ravaging her in desperation, in passion.

"Fuck me harder Travis," she whispered. "Show me."

Her words rang into my ears and needed no further explanation. Her breath was hot against my neck, and her legs relaxed. She opened herself to me as much as possible, and I spun her back around, tossing her down onto the bed. I drove my cock deep into her, and she squirmed on the comforter, balling it up in one hand as my fingers wrapped tightly around her waist.

I pulled her in with each thrust and felt myself edging closer losing control. She was shaking and convulsing under me, her body roiling through climax after climax, and I was relentless. I needed the release as much as she did, to put an exclamation point on the words that we said. This was the proof, the evidence of how perfect we were for another. Our bodies fit like they were designed for the other, and only the other. Her body was a perfect illustration of beauty in the throes of passion. I craved her, even while inside her. I wanted more. I would always want more.

The tension was building as I slammed into her as fast and hard as I could. I knew it would be over soon, and I yearned for that moment of release. Of the kind of absolute, soul completion that only she could bring from me. Her eyes had rolled in the back of her head, but suddenly they were back, aware and staring into mine. Staring directly into my soul.

"Please," she mumbled. "With me."

My mind went blank with desire. Her voice filled the room around me, and suddenly I found my own among the chorus. The tension built and snapped, and I exploded into her. Her body locked up under mine, and our foreheads touched as I emptied myself into her. She drew every drop from my body, and I shook as I ran dry. It was the most powerful climax in my life, and I collapsed into her arms on my bed. Curling her naked body around me, I pulled the blanket over us. Our lips crushed into each other, and she sighed as she settled her head into the center of my chest.

Our hearts beat together as we lazily reveled in our skin touching and our souls mending.

EPILOGUE

TRAVIS - THREE YEARS LATER...

The ring was burning a hole in my pocket.

My leg bounced as I waited through all the Christmas events and pulled people aside as needed. It was nerve-racking, but I made it through. Just a little bit of time left to go. All the hard stuff was over, except the last bit. Of course, that was the one I was most nervous about. I shouldn't be. I knew she was going to say yes. But I was still out of my mind nervous about it.

In the three years since I had come back, our little family had grown closer and tighter. Amelia had been the first person I pulled aside. At nine years old, she was good for a little conspiratorial silliness with her dad. On a night where Carrie was out with Tina doing Christmas shopping, I had shown Amelia the ring and told her my plan. She was over the moon about it. It was everything she wanted, and now it was going to be official. For too long, she had been denied a full family, and then when I did come home and entered her life, there was always that question as to what was going to happen when my residency ended.

This very question had been answered the morning I

told Amelia I was going to ask Carrie to marry me. The hospital was seeing a lot more patients and needed the help full-time if I would take it. I signed on and would be starting as a full-fledged employee on the first day of February. I was still on call during the Christmas break, but after working through just about every other holiday and not taking a vacation, they insisted I take time off before I became an employee. It meant over a month off, starting on Christmas Eve. Amelia was delighted.

That's why I was sitting at home, our new home, when I told her parents what I was planning on.

We had invited them to our place, the first time they had celebrated Christmas not in their own home since Carrie's grandparents passed, and they had agreed. The new house still had some rooms that had boxes still packed, but for the most part it was put together. Carrie had been a little slow in putting things up since she was pregnant again, and I had been busy at work and then dealing with selling my parents' old place. Hank had offered to help me get it in sellable shape, and he and I had been working on it for the better part of two years.

When I told her parents, they were both effusive in their approval, wrapping me up in hugs. Her father apologized again, for what must have been the hundredth time, for how he had treated me when we were younger and his role in me running away to the East Coast. We had a rough go at first when I came back, but water was under the bridge now, and they were elated to see that their daughter would be walking down the aisle with me.

Since we had the big new house and I had the time off, the annual New Year's Eve party was going to be bigger and better than ever. I decided after the party would be the perfect time to propose.

Several of my coworker friends came by as did a bunch of Carrie's friends from around town. Hank and Tina tag teamed keeping Amelia entertained while we filtered in and out of the rooms of the house with our guests. Then, a sleepy nine-year-old holding my hand, we rang in the new year.

It was three in the morning now, and the last of the partiers had made their way out of the door. The ones who chose not to drink were driving those who had, and the few who didn't have rides or didn't want to wait had a rideshare called for them. When the last straggler was gone, I closed the door and turned to look around the remains of the party.

For the most part, the house was clean, just decorations still in some areas. Tina and Hank had helped us by taking most of it down on their way out, and Amelia had been crashed on the couch since about one-thirty. She still had a little party hat on when she went down, and I had to gently remove it while she slept so it didn't choke her. She slept by the light of the Christmas tree that was still up in the living room, its twinkling red and green lights giving a cozy feeling that I wanted to last forever.

Carrie was in the kitchen, cleaning up the last remnants of the mess made by the party. Figuring that the mood wouldn't be terribly great if she was worried about the house, I picked up the bottles and glasses in the living room and dining room and tossed what needed to go out. When the room seemed like all it needed anymore was a wipe down and a vacuum, I made my way into the kitchen.

Carrie danced to the slow jazz music playing in the background as she washed a dish and put it in the drainer. I walked up behind her and wrapped my arms around her waist. She stopped and turned into me, and we danced in the kitchen for a few moments, her head rested on my arm.

Sighing happily, Carrie kissed my neck, and I knew this was the moment. I stepped back from her, and for a moment she looked confused as I knelt down.

"Are you okay?" she asked, then gasped as she realized I was on one knee and had a box in one hand. "Oh, Travis," she said, her voice warbling on the edge of tears.

"I know we are just in our kitchen, cleaning up after our friends, but I honestly don't think there is a better time to do this than now," I said, opening the box. "Carrie Jacobs, will you marry me?"

Tears streamed down her face as she nodded and hoarsely whispered, "Yes, yes!"

I slid the ring on her finger and then stood, and she collapsed into me with her lips pressing against mine and her arms wrapping tight around my waist. When our kiss broke, I looked deeply into her eyes and brushed away a tear from her cheek.

"I love you," I said.

"I love you too," she responded.

Wild applause suddenly filled the room, and we both turned to see the elated face of Amelia popping her head up over the bar and clapping with all her might. I waved her in, and she ran toward us, arms outstretched.

Barreling into us, she nearly knocked Carrie over, but I held them in place and we hugged tightly. Together, we stayed that way for a good little bit of time, Carrie sneaking kisses to me occasionally, before finally going off to bed. I finally had a family to be proud of.

The End

Made in the USA
Middletown, DE
25 September 2021